The
Melancholy
Moon

Glenda C. Manus

Library of Congress Cataloging-in-Publication
Data is on file with the publisher

Text copyright © 2016 by Glenda Manus
Published in 2016 by South Ridge Press

ISBN-13:978-1532714573
ISBN-10:1532714572

Printed in the United States of America
10 9 8 7 6 5 4 3 2 1 BP 24 23 22 21 20 19 18 17 16

Cover Designer: Greg Banks

Second Edition

This is a work of fiction. Any resemblance to any
actual person, living or dead, business
establishments, events or locales is strictly
coincidental.

A Special Thank You

To my editors, Laura Whittaker and Krista Cook for their eagle eyes and helpful suggestions.

To my friends and family for believing in me.

To my readers for their sweet words of encouragement.

And especially to God, whose gentle prodding takes me to places I would never dare to go alone.

John 8:36
If the Son sets you free, you will really be free.

More Books by this author:
Sweet Tea and Southern Grace
Lighting the Way
High Tide at Pelican Pointe

The Melancholy Moon

A Sweet Tea Mystery

Glenda C. Manus

CHAPTER 1

The white rental cottage sits on the edge of the water at the mouth of the Lockwood Folly River, barely a stone's throw from Oak Island. It's a simple little cottage with a porch on the front side and a large deck on the water side. It's a beachy sort of place built in the '50's with white clapboard siding, shutters as blue as the sky, and a gazebo built right upon the water as an afterthought. I loved that gazebo the first time I laid eyes upon it, but I couldn't foresee that it would be my saving grace; a place where I would find solace in the face of fearing the unknown, the fear of death, and later, a place where I would pick up the pieces of a heart, long ago broken and learn how to love and laugh again.

Eleanor and I had rented it for the summer; or at least part of the summer; July and August, a time that she would coddle and care for me more like a mother than a sister.

The gazebo is built on stilts, with the outer posts hugging the bank and no matter how the sun is positioned in the sky, it seems to be always making shadows over the water. Heat waves form at the water's surface and rise into the sizzling summer air creating a shimmering effect. It makes the posts look as if they're dancing around, trying to tempt the tide to rise high enough to pull their skinny little legs out to sea. The sun reflecting off the dock onto the blue water below refracts into patterns that can make you quite dizzy if you stare at it long enough. I would sit for hours watching all this, along with the small silver minnows flipping the surface, only to be swept up and swallowed by the seabirds perched patiently upon dock pilings, their vertical supports sunk deep into the waterway bottom. I could see my own small rental boat rise in the water with each swell, raising it up and plopping it back down again alongside the floating dock where it was moored. Those soft water sounds have always been comforting to me. They bring a feeling of contentment like nothing else I've ever experienced. But for those of us who have had to pick ourselves up off the floor after a divorce, death of a loved one, or a lengthy illness, contentment doesn't last and can sometimes be replaced by cynicism and distrust. I often find myself thinking of all the conflicted emotions I felt while spending our summer by the sea. Anger, worry, sadness, defeatism to name a few. But there was also joy, laughter and love. And love is sometimes a silly and fickle thing.

***

The last round of chemo had royally kicked my butt, and I have to admit there were times I had second thoughts about my decision to stay alive. Upchucking, dry heaving and constant nausea isn't and never has been on my list of favorite things. When I was first diagnosed, I asked Simon, my oncologist, if I was going to live or die from the cancer that attached itself like a leech to my left ovary. He just looked at me solemnly.

"Spit it out", I said. "I need to know."

"I have to wait until I do the surgery before I can stage it."

"Stage it?" I had no idea what he meant.

"Yes, staging it means seeing how far advanced it is. I'll need to see if it's spread outside the ovary so we can determine how to treat it. That'll also give us a better estimate on the odds of beating it. But ovarian cancer in any stage is not good."

"I love your optimism, Simon," I said. "It makes for such a charming bedside manner. What other choice do I have?" I could see he picked up on my attitude, but in his defense, he kept his cool. I suppose my sense of snarkiness has developed from too much time alone. My country club friends think it's cute and eccentric, but my family doesn't let me get away with it too often.

"Cassie, this is invasive epithelial ovarian cancer." He said it in a way that stressed each word separately, like he was talking to a child. He held my hand and his sad eyes looked straight into mine. "Invasive is the key word here. Your other choice is probably a year... tops." Not exactly what I wanted to hear.

"Uh!" I looked long and hard at my brother, his shoulders visibly drooping. I could tell it was killing him to give me this news. "Well, that was a blunt way of putting it. What a way to make up my mind in a hurry. When do we start?"

***

The day after surgery, Simon sat on the side of my hospital bed.

"It's late stage two," he said, "not good but better than most patients I see. Most of the time, it's found too late."

"What are my odds?"

"It's hard to tell. I've had quite a few patients who've survived stage four.... But then again, I've also had some die of the earlier stages."

"Is that the best you can tell me? You're waffling, Simon. How about yes or no, live or die? I want something in writing."

"Cassie, be quiet for a minute and listen to me, and no, I'm not waffling. Patients respond to chemotherapy differently. What works for some may not work for others. A complete response, which is what we're hoping for, means that all the cancer or tumor disappears. A partial response means the cancer has shrunk but the disease remains. Then there's also a stable response and a disease progression, but we won't get into those right now. The good news is the five-year survival rate at this stage is about 60 to 75%, and you're at an age where the odds are in your favor."

It didn't faze him that I had yelled at him. He's grown accustomed to it over the years.

"You'll have to have aggressive chemo. It's not in your lymph nodes, but there are still some small cells in the abdominal wall. I'm almost certain the chemo will kill these cells, but it's going to be rough on you."

Simon is my brother, the only boy out of four doorstep children in our family - the smartest one of us by far, although we girls like to say we didn't try as hard. We were far too busy looking for potential husbands. But what Simon lacks in his bedside manner, he makes up for in pure brilliance.

***

He removed the right ovary along with the cancerous one. My fallopian tubes and uterus were also removed. Standard procedure, he told me. It didn't matter to me. I was past childbearing years and I had never wanted kids anyway. It's a good thing because I don't think I could have had any. Stan had wanted children badly. To carry on the Smith name he said. And why? I had asked him. There are too many Smiths in the world as it is.

That's the reason he left me. Not because of the too many Smiths comment, but because of no children. Sure, he said it was our irreconcilable differences as his lawyer had instructed him to say, but I knew it was because I couldn't produce a boy child - or any child at all apparently. It hurt, but as with all hurts, they fade with time. He married Darlene, a pretty little gold digger fifteen years younger than both of us. That was fourteen years ago. Darlene had given him something I couldn't, three little girls, and he didn't seem to mind one whit that they wouldn't keep the Smith name going. Beautiful girls they were, just like their mother who turned out to be just right for old Stanley. I no longer missed him, but I was still resentful about being jilted.

Since our arrival at the cottage, I had settled into a routine, trying to regain my strength. I would walk down the short flight of stairs to the docks where seafood houses and shrimp boats lined the waterway. If I got up early enough, I took the rental boat out and tried my hand at fishing. Most days, I just enjoyed the beauty of nature all around me, the marsh birds, turtles and snakes in their natural habitat, and the smell of salty sea air. I began to think of the house as an old comfortable friend, like the place where I grew up. Even though the side effects of chemo were playing havoc with my body, I was fairly content with the routine until one particular day that changed everything. I had sat all morning on the gazebo with a book, a notebook and a pen, sometimes reading, sometimes writing, but mostly just watching the boats go by.

"Cassie, come on in for lunch."

It was Eleanor, my oldest sister - older than me by six years. Like I said, we were doorsteps - Eleanor, Penny, Simon and me, spread out over a six-year period. Our mama said we would've been closer together, but she breastfed each of us as long as she could to delay the inevitable. She was a baby making machine. She was also very clever. After I was born, she got busy and decorated one of the bedrooms with pinks and greens, spending a small fortune on bedding, drapes and new carpet. Daddy was under the assumption that the remodeled room was going to be for Eleanor and Penny. Then Mama claimed it for herself, never moving back into Daddy's bedroom except for an occasional tryst after she finally discovered birth control was available. I often wonder if Eleanor would be an only child if 'the pill' had made its way to the backwoods of the Low Country earlier. Mama didn't seem particularly fond of children. Oh, she loved us - there was no doubt of that, but she usually left us to our own devises, not wanting to be bothered. It was the way things were done in her wealthy little world growing up. At least her own mother had hired a nanny for her children. But Mother married Daddy and left the rich world behind.

"You do want lunch, don't you?" Eleanor's voice showed her concern, just as it had since I was diagnosed three months earlier.

"Yes, sorry - my mind was a million miles away."

"That's quite a long journey," she said. "I'm surprised you made it back so fast."

I smiled. She'd been trying so hard to get me to eat. When she found out I had lost twenty-five pounds in such a short time, she put her foot down, saying "We're going somewhere - a nice and calm place - just me and you so I can fatten you up." And that's how we ended up in Varnamtown, an odd name for a little village that sits right smack in the middle of fish houses and shrimp boats.

"What's for lunch?" I asked.

"A grilled cheese sandwich, sliced tomatoes and a can of peaches." By trial and error, we had narrowed down the foods that are the least likely to make me sick. I knew I wouldn't be able to eat the tomato, but I would try to get the rest down. Her desire for me to get well, and my desire to please her was my driving force.

"Why don't we eat out here on the gazebo?" I asked. "There's a great breeze and I love watching the boats go by."

"Good idea, hold tight and I'll bring it out on a tray. I may need to reheat the grilled cheese because of your daydreaming. Is sweet tea okay?"

"My favorite," I said. She went back inside. I had been drinking unsweetened tea for years, trying every little thing to hold my weight in check. The only good thing I found about having cancer was that I could finally drink or eat all the sugar I wanted and not gain an ounce. And sugar was about the only thing I had an appetite for. My cancer was craving it. My cancer; I guess I should've given it a name, like Polly or Sam or something, because it seemed to have a life of its own. Even though most of it had been whacked out, the remainder felt sort of like an evil twin sitting on my shoulder.

Before I got sick, I had weighed a hundred and fifty pounds, which was a bit much for my 5'6" frame, but I'd always stayed in good shape, worked out at the gym, and carried it well. One-twenty-five shows as an ideal weight on the charts, but it made me look like the walking dead. Of course, my body being poisoned wasn't helping my appearance at all, but now that I was over a week into a month long reprieve from chemo, my appetite was returning... almost.

The stray cat that we had named Raphael jumped up on my lap and startled me. He had an uncanny way of looking into my face and blinking in rapid succession. "What do you want now, cat?" I asked him. I'm not familiar with cat language, but when I would rub behind his ears, it seemed to satisfy him. He and I watched as a family in a small boat threw out an anchor right below where we were sitting. The man patiently put bait on the young girl's hook and threw it out. He then started to put bait on the boy's, who was even younger. "Let me do it," the boy asked. "Please?" The man paused for a minute, looking from the sharp hook to the dead stinky shrimp, then at the boy. I was surprised when he gave in. Hooks and kids don't mix - a lesson I remember from my early days of fishing. After a couple of attempts, I heard a loud, "Ouch", and the boy threw the shrimp down and grabbed his finger.

I understood what the dad had done. It's one of those life lessons I had just learned. Sometimes you have to let people figure things out on their own so they can get it into their hard heads that they need help. Like me.

Eleanor had wanted to help from the very beginning of my treatments. I could go stay at her place, she offered, but I said no because I didn't want to inconvenience her. I didn't tell her that though. I told her I would be more comfortable at home. Then she offered to come stay with me. Her husband, Blake, works out of town except on weekends, and could easily come visit. That left me with no excuse, so I told her the truth; that I've been independent for sixteen years and I could do this alone. How dumb of me. I quickly found out I couldn't. She stayed with me two weeks as I recovered from surgery, but I sent her home after that and I made out okay through the first few weeks of treatment thanks to my friends in Raleigh. But with each successive treatment I grew weaker and finally realized I couldn't take advantage of my friends. They were getting tired of it anyway and had started dropping out like flies, so I had no choice but to take Eleanor up on her offer.

When she mentioned the little seaport town with the tiny cottage sitting so close to the water's edge, I felt as if I was being offered an oasis in the middle of a dessert. I jumped at the chance because I had finally figured out that I would just wallow in self-pity and die of malnutrition if I didn't have someone to force feed me.

***

The little family of four in the boat had no idea I was watching them. The walls of the gazebo are high and it was rare to be spotted by any of the boats passing by. Even the times I stood and looked over the railing, no one seemed to notice me. Eleanor teased me and said my straw colored hair was camouflaged by the tall marsh grass that glows like the color of wheat in the fields when the sun shines upon it. I thought it was just because my sickness had made me invisible, so her description cheered me up somewhat. I was thankful that I hadn't lost my hair, although it was a lot duller than my normal dark blonde. Simon seemed to be more surprised than anyone else. My hair was my one small vanity and it was still clinging to life, just as I was.

***

"It isn't much," Eleanor said, shooing the cat off my lap. She put the silver tray on the table in front of me. It's just like Eleanor to serve a grilled cheese sandwich on a sterling silver tray, one that she brought for special occasions. The tomato was peeled and cut into little wedges, and the peaches were in a crystal parfait cup with whipped cream on top. Every day is a special occasion for my sister, the optimist in our family. Thank God for optimists.

"It's perfect", I said, and meant it. Suddenly I was ravenous and I made short work of the sandwich and peaches, leaving only the crust of the bread on my plate. I pushed the tomato around on the small china saucer, but couldn't bring myself to eat it. Eleanor was delighted with what I did eat and scrambled up from her half-eaten grilled cheese.

"Can I fix you another one? How about more tea?"

"Sit back down and eat, Eleanor. I can't hold another bite. If you keeping hopping around like that, you're going to be the one losing weight. I'm not helpless."

She sat back down with a sigh. "I know", she said, and commenced to eat her sandwich. I let the crust of my sandwich slip out of my hand to the floor, unnoticed by Eleanor. Raphael was waiting patiently at my feet and devoured it as soon as it hit the deck. The cat weighed at least twenty pounds, but his pathetic meow made you think he was starved. I'm sure he'd used that trick many times on the dock and around the fish houses.

***

The wind picked up and we watched as clouds rolled in from the east. Everything around us seemed to lose its glitter. The water suddenly changed from a sparkling blue to a dull grey when the sun disappeared behind the clouds. The marsh grass was no longer shining. A weather bulletin must have been issued because boats started scurrying in from the sea to take their place in line at the landing. Trucks with trailers started to queue up to pull them out one by one. The locals pulled their boats into their assigned slips, tied them down to the floating dock and made a mad dash for the covered boardwalk attached to the fish house. They would wait out the storm, gathering there for a little fish talk and proudly displaying what they had caught thus far.

Eleanor gathered up our trays and turned to go inside. "You should come on in; you'll get wet."

"I think I'll stay out here for a while and watch the rain. Anyway, I'm not sweet enough to melt." It was a silly cliche, I know, but it was what we siblings had said about each other since forever. They said it about me the most, since I was always the impish one, following my daddy everywhere, even more so than Simon, his only boy.

"I'll come in if it gets bad." And I would have, because there's nothing that scares me more than thunder and lighting.

Now Eleanor, on the other hand, probably would melt, just like the sugar cube she puts in her coffee each morning from the little sterling spoon. She's the elegant one, having been trained in the social graces by the Southern matriarch herself, the late departed Isabella Richfield Davenport, our filthy rich maternal grandmother. Eleanor is truly sweet though, being amazingly unaffected by our arrogant Grandmother Bella.

The rain started really coming down and the wind was blowing it sideways into the gazebo. I don't give up easily but I'm not overly fond of getting drenched, so I stood up and readied myself to run from the cover of the gazebo across the open porch and into the house. Before I made my dash, I heard a boat motor and looked down just in time to see a boat try to pull into the slip next to mine. The slip I rent is designed for two boats, and as I watched helplessly, the wind and waves caused the other boat to slam hard against the starboard side of my rented boat as the driver tried to maneuver it in place.

"What are you trying to do?" I yelled down. "You're gonna sink my boat!"

The man jumped out of his boat and looked up. A pair of deep blue eyes stared at me from under the visor of an army green parka. "I'm sorry! It got away from me. I don't think there's any harm done, but if there is, I have insurance." He tied the rope tightly to the mooring, then turned back to me. "I'll be right up." I heard his footsteps pound on the boards as he took the stairs two at a time, and in a flash he was right there beside me, taking up the majority of the space under the gazebo and seemingly right in my face.

I don't like to share my space with much of anybody, so I stepped back. The blue eyes were still way too close for comfort, and I gulped, suddenly at a loss for words. Me, Cassandra Arnett Phillips, at a loss for words. No way! I tried to get all huffed up and indignant. Those danged blue eyes. I should have gone inside when Eleanor told me to.

The parka came off and he held out his hand. "Carl McGee. I'm pleased to make your acquaintance."

I was hoping he would be obnoxious and maybe a Yankee so that I could be snarly and yell at him again. I didn't count on him being polite and a Southerner to boot. It had been on the tip of my tongue to tell him he should have been more careful, but now it would sound petty. I didn't have much of a choice but to hold my hand out too. "Cassie Phillips", I said begrudgingly, and jerked my hand back as soon as he shook it.

"Hey, you're getting soaked." He looked up at the roof of the gazebo and spotted the hooks where I sometimes hang a mesh screen to filter out the blazing sun while I'm trying to write. He hung his parka from one hook to the other on the side where the wind was blowing the rain in upon us. Aha, cute and smart too. I wouldn't have thought to do that. He looked around and in one sweeping glance seemed to take in the scene completely, including me from head to toe. "Do you live here?" he asked.

"No, we're just renting it for a couple of months."

"Me too. I'm renting the grey house next door. I'm just now bringing my boat down from Wrightsville Beach and some friends are bringing my truck tomorrow."

"Why were you out in this storm?" I said it accusingly and he didn't miss the inflection, but he laughed.

"Well, I didn't plan on a storm when I started out," he said. "Storms have a way of sneaking up on you out here on the water in hot weather. One minute the sun was shining, and the next minute a monsoon hit me." He looked from the gazebo to the house. "You got caught in it too, I see. How were you planning to get back inside without getting wet?"

"I won't melt," I said for the second time in the last ten minutes. This time it sounded kind of lame.

"Maybe your husband will come out and rescue you." Did I detect a bit of snarkiness bouncing right back at me?

"I don't need rescuing," I said, probably a little too curtly. The blue eyes held mine for a minute, then looked away.

"No, I don't guess you do." He saw the notebook on the little shelf under the glass top table and grabbed it. He turned a few pages, stopping at one point to read, then turned again until he found a clean sheet. He pulled out his wallet from his jeans pocket. "Here's my insurance information just in case there's any damage to your boat." He started writing, paused a moment to think, then with a faint smile finished writing, closed the notebook and put it back under the table. Keeping his eyes averted, he grabbed the parka and pulled it over his head. "I'll see ya' later," he said, and made a run for it, down the steps to the wet pavement below.

I watched as he loped off in the direction of the grey house; then watched as he walked up the steps to his porch, shucking his parka and hanging it on a nail before he walked inside.

"Why do I always have to be such a witch?" I said out loud.

Just then the door opened and Eleanor stuck her head out. "Come on in Cassie. I don't want you getting sick on me. Your immune system is down."

And why did she have to remind me? For the last few minutes, I hadn't given my immune system a single thought. Maybe having a neighbor would get me out of the funk I was in.

The rain stopped as quickly as it had started. I grabbed my notebook and walked across the porch with blue eyes on my mind. I almost tripped on Raphael as he scooted in before me.

CHAPTER 2

The clouds and rain continued, allowing only a few teasing rays of sunshine throughout the day. I love rainy days with nothing to do. One thing Eleanor and I have in common is we both love to read. We spent many an hour as kids reading in her bedroom long past our parents' night time command of "last call for lights out." Penny and I shared a room, but she hated to read and wanted total darkness after lights out. I would take my book and sneak across the hall into Eleanor's room. We would stuff a blanket to cover the space under the door where no light would shine through, then we would read to our heart's content in comfortable silence except for tears and sniffles at the sad parts and laughs out loud at the funny parts. Sometimes I would fall asleep and wake up with the sharp corners of either my book or hers digging into my back.

We're still like that and on this day I was stretched out on the sofa and she in the recliner, both with books in our hands. One drawback of being a writer is you never have time to leisurely read a book. I've learned to read in small snatches here and there. Writing has been my life for the last twelve years and my agent expects me to write day and night. She wasn't happy at the "Big C" diagnosis, especially after my brain couldn't pump out the words due to the chemo doing its little tricks in there. I finally drilled it into her head that I was taking a few months off and would start back only if I lived. That got her attention and she left me alone. Agents aren't crazy about writers who don't have the potential to keep the books flowing, and I wouldn't be much good if I was dead.

I picked up my notebook that morning though, and I began to write. The thoughts didn't come easy, but they came with more clarity than I'd had in a couple of months. I felt in the groove again, even if it was only a temporary reprieve from chemo brain.

The book I chose to read wasn't calling to me like it should. I like to get completely immersed in a book, so much so that if the fire department is banging on my door to get inside, I would absent-mindedly get up, open the door and ask them to let me know when they've put out the fire. This one was so slow that the cat jumping on my lap was enough diversion for me to put the book down and fold his ears over, then rub them softly between my fingers so he'd flip over on his back and purr. There's something so relaxing about rubbing a cat's ears, for the cat and for me. It put him sound asleep.

I stretched out my arm, hoping to reach my notebook without falling off the sofa and waking Raphael. I looked over what I'd written and was pleased with how it was shaping up. I had already decided to write something very different from my normal genre. Steamy romance was the farthest thing from my mind right then. I was thinking more like a campfire that has fizzled out. This book would be a soft love story, something tender; and if my agent didn't like tender, then I'd find another agent. Or better still, self-publish. My contract with the agency was expiring soon and I was too sick to worry about renewing it. I've built up a following over the years and my name recognition would be enough to carry my book to a small, even though unadvertised, success. Hopefully.

I'd only written one chapter in the notebook, and as I flipped through the pages and got to the end, I saw a bold handwriting that wasn't mine, and it shocked me for a moment that someone else had written in my notebook. Then I laughed out loud when I saw what he wrote. He must have noticed that I was writing the makings of a book or short story, because he wrote the new page in the same fashion. Centered in the middle of the page was the 'book title' and it read; Shipwrecked by Carl McGee. Then it listed his insurance information much like a copyright or disclaimer page. "Names, characters, locations, incidents and accidents are strictly coincidental, but if they prove to be otherwise you may call Crowley Insurance Agency at 1-800-622-4141." Then he proceeded to give his policy number as an ISBN number. I laughed again. I liked his sense of humor and he knew more than a little bit about books. I was intrigued. The memory of those piercing blue eyes came back to me and I sighed, apparently loudly.

"What is it?" Eleanor asked. "First laughter, then a sultry sigh." She glanced at my notebook. "You must be writing another romance."

I stammered and blushed, something I don't think I've ever done in my entire life, and I closed the notebook. "Uh, no. I'm writing something a little lighter this time." I didn't want to admit that I was a little bit moonstruck, and I resolve to toughen up. I wouldn't allow myself to be vulnerable ever again.

I thought about Stan and how hurt and betrayed I felt when he left. Thinking of the betrayal always helped bolster my resolve not to get involved again. Stan and I still had a connection of sorts - money. We were still civil to one another, even though he did screw me over royally when he started his affair with Darlene while we were still married. Even though we couldn't conceive, I thought we were fairly happy and were destined to grow old together since we rarely argued. Come to think of it, that's pretty boring in and of itself. Just as in writing a book, you have to put a little conflict in the story or the reader, or in our case, the participants, will be bored to death.

But he was paying for his sins - monetarily at least. $6000 a month until I remarried or was financially stable on my own. His lawyer, who thought he was so clever, was asleep on that issue. Why do you think I never remarried? I may be a little wacky, but I'm not stupid. And financially stable? Hah - that's a joke. I'm a writer and writers don't get rich - not unless you're Pat Conroy, Danielle Steele, Stephen King or... that writer who wrote the Harry Potter books. I found it hard to remember her name because of my chemo fried brain. I've never read any of her books anyway, so that's a good excuse not to know her name. I don't care for reading about wizards and muggles, whatever they are.

I write romance novels - the hot and steamy ones, as if I know something about hot and steamy romance stuff. Not the x-rated kind of books, but not for the faint of heart either. My publishers have made plenty of money off my novels, but by the time they take their chunk of change, there's not a whole lot left for me.

Anyway, it wasn't hurting Stan one bit to shell out my monthly allowance, and really, he never complained much about it. His daddy died and left him megabucks and a large family business to run. Nope, $6000 a month is peanuts to him, but I would have been lost without it.

"Cassie?"

"Hmm, what?" I turned around and found my sister staring at me. Sometimes it catches me off guard at how pretty she is, the only one of us with dark hair and brown eyes, taking after our maternal grandmother. The rest of us having varying shades of blondish brown hair and green eyes like our father's side of the family.

"You're daydreaming again. I'm trying to talk to you."

"Well, talk on Sis, you've got my attention now."

"Who was the guy that came up on the porch during the storm?"

So she had seen him. I thought it was my little secret since she hadn't mentioned it until then.

"He manhandled my boat as he was docking his and I yelled at him. He seems to have no idea how to handle a boat in a storm."

She gave me the older sister look, slipping her reading glasses down over her nose. "Could you have done any better? The storm came up fast, and the combination of a high tide, the wind and the choppy water, it's hard to control a boat in such a small slip. You know that."

She was right, of course, but I knew I could have done better. I've been driving a boat since I was ten, or as our daddy always said, knee-high to a grasshopper.

"Whatever." It was my new favorite word. "I just wanted to get his insurance information in case the rental boat is damaged. You know how they go over rental stuff when you turn it back in." She continued with the glasses on the nose scare tactic and was still looking at me in that accusatory kind of way. "Anyway, we're stuck with him. He's rented the grey house for the summer."

"I'm sure he's a very nice man." Then she gave me another evil eye. "Were you mean to him, Cassie? Like you're mean to every tall, dark and handsome man you've come across since you divorced Stan?"

I swear, those glasses go down a little farther and her eyebrows arch a little sharper each time she scolds me. "I am not mean. I'm just....wary." We both laughed. Since my divorce, eligible men seemed to bring out the worst in me. It was a good defense tactic.

"Whatever," she mumbled, and I laughed. The word is addicting.

CHAPTER 3

My bedroom in the little white house wasn't much bigger than my bathroom at home. It was all I needed though. It made me long for one of those little houses that are all the rage now. It would force me to get rid of all the stuff I don't need and live simply. There was a double bed, a little nightstand and a small dresser. Miniature furniture, and all of it painted red. The paneled walls were painted white and the curtains were navy blue with a border of red checks. A vintage oar hung over the bed. It was more of a boyish decor, but cheerful. After my teeth were brushed and flossed, I washed my face and then downed my nausea pill. I looked in the mirror and examined my face. Without makeup, I looked washed out. The few freckles scattered across my nose stood out against my white skin. I wondered if I should work on a tan - just enough to give me a little natural color. But then again, sun exposure without sunscreen can cause cancer and I don't need any more of that.

People have always told me I'm pretty, but for the life of me, I've never seen it. My hair is almost to my waist and slightly curly. When I wear it in a ponytail, little wisps of hair fall down around my temples and I keep examining it to see if it's turning grey. So far, so good. If I could just hold on to it through all the chemo, it could turn white or grey or blue for all I cared. But what I really wanted was for it to stay attached to my head.

I lay in bed for a while, ready for sleep but it wasn't ready for me. My mind replayed the events of the afternoon.

The rain stopped in mid-afternoon and the sun came out, and it came out blazing hot with barely a breeze wafting through the windows. We'd been lucky so far. The house was built with good ventilation. With all the windows open, it caught the good coastal breezes and we had used the air conditioning only a handful of times. That afternoon, Eleanor gave in and turned it on. With no fat on my bones I'm always cold, so to keep from freezing I went for a walk. The docks were full of shrimp boats, coming north from McClellanville and south from Pamlico Sound. More and more boats were harvesting offshore in the big water because they'd closed some of the rivers to shrimping. When this happens it puts a lot of little shrimp boats out of business because they're not equipped for big water. The economy of these little seaport towns is so dependent upon the shrimp industry; from the shrimpers themselves to the fish houses that sell the shrimp and other bycatch. It's no wonder so many shrimp boats are dry docked and the beautiful and peaceful marshes that have been in the same families for more than a century are being sold to developers that build mini-castles to sell to water-obsessed rich people.

The locals were surprisingly friendly to me and Eleanor, and in the short time we were there, we bought enough shrimp from the fish house, that we were on a first name basis. You'd think that growing up in the South Carolina Lowcountry, we'd be tired of shrimp, but

I could eat it every day - well, every day that I'm not sick anyway.

Eleanor gave me a trash bag to carry to the large trash can designated as ours - number 10. Someone had written the number on the dark grey can with white paint. There was a sticker placed on the can with the trash pickup schedule and I read it. Wednesdays and Saturdays, and I had just missed it. I put the trash bag on the ground for a moment as I gathered momentum to throw the heavy thing in the can. Inside was a bread bag with two remaining end slices. Eleanor never uses end slices - wasteful! If I don't eat them, I save them for the birds or the fish in my Koi pond back home. I pulled the bread bag out, and after taking a deep breath, hoisted the heavy bag up and in the can. I wouldn't have thought it heavy at all a few months back, pre-surgery and pre-chemo. Before I could get the lid back on a yellow jacket came storming out of the can. Calm and easy, Cassie, I said to myself, and resisted the urge to run. It worked. He ignored me and started trying to finagle his way back into the can.

After strolling around the neighborhood for a while, I made my way back to the gazebo. I crumbled the bread and threw one tiny piece into the water. A small mud minnow came to the surface and devoured it, followed quickly by a larger Pogie who in turn devoured the mud minnow. It's funny how one small crumb can interrupt the cycle of life. One small crumb.

I think of the devil throwing whole slices out to those of us gullible enough to snatch them up. And cancer! It's like all the bread in the bakery. It was so hard not to think of it constantly, because it was thriving on my feeding it. Like a stain that grows larger with the washing. Shakespeare. I played the part of Lady McBeth in high school drama class two years in a row.

"Out damned spot, out, I say!" I realized I said it aloud and looked around to make sure no one was watching, and then looked down at the boat where I planned to go next to check for scratches. A pair of blue eyes met mine and they twinkled as they held my own.

"Feeding the fish and quoting Shakespeare - you're a woman of many talents."

I looked around for something heavy to throw at him, but changed my mind. He would probably think I was flirting. I tried out my best smirk but it fell short. "Just practicing what I'm going to say when I see the big dent you put in my boat."

He wasn't the least bit insulted. He shrugged and held his arms out. "I've checked it out already and there's not so much as a scratch." I raised my eyebrows. "Come on down and check it out if you don't believe me."

Bracing myself for an up close encounter with those eyes, I stomped down the stairs like I was fifty shades of aggravated. I made a point not to look in the eyes, but instead bent down and closely examined where our boats were almost touching. I checked it, front to back. No scratches. Conceding there was no damage, I got back up to tell him so.

With a swift movement, he flecked something off my shoulder and I panicked. "Is it a bee?" I asked, brushing my shoulder and swatting at my hair. "I'm allergic to bees."

"No," he says, "it was a small chip."

I was confused for a moment but then I got it. I laughed so hard I had to sit down on the bottom step until I could get control. When I looked up, I found him watching me in amusement. "Touche," I said, getting up and wiping my sweaty hands on the legs of my rumpled khaki shorts.

"Let's try this again." I reached out my hand. "Hi, I'm Cassie."

He took my hand in his. "Glad to meet you, Cassie. I'm Carl."

In the deep recesses of my mind, I was scolding myself. "What kind of mess are you getting yourself into, Cassandra Phillips?" But I didn't answer myself. I was too busy drowning in a pool of blue eyes that were equally as busy looking into mine.

I've replayed the handshake in my mind a dozen times. It was only a brief touch, but it felt a little like the time I put a bobby pin in an electric socket when Mama wasn't watching.

I sure wasn't going to get to sleep with thoughts like that, so I turned over and grabbed one of the pillows, turning it to the cooler side. I settled back down, hoping that sleep would find me.

CHAPTER 4

I slept long and hard but dreamed most of the night. I keep a notebook beside my bed and if a dream wakes me up, I'll put on my reading glasses and write it down. You never know when you're going to need a goofy dream in your story, and I'll forget them in a flash if I don't make a note of them. No matter how much I try to convince myself that I'll remember them, I never can.

The last dream woke me up at 6 a.m. Stan's wife was pulling me by my hair down a long hallway. I knew she had carried a grudge all these years because I got such a hefty alimony sum, but this was ridiculous. My hair actually hurt when I came fully awake. Dreams are crazy like that. I took it as a sign to go ahead and get up since I planned to take the boat out anyway.

With my favorite rod and reel and a cup of coffee in a thermos, I hopped aboard the boat. It was a nice little boat with a 50 hp engine and it started right up. Morning is the best time to explore the little creeks and coves along the waterway. There's no boat traffic except for the hardcore fishermen looking for mud minnows and menhaden around the docks and pilings. I just watch the seagulls. With their aerial view and keen eyesight, they'll show you exactly where the bait fish are by their noisy diving in and out of the water catching a few for themselves. After casting my net a few times, I caught all the mud minnows I needed. I even shared a few with a vacationing rookie fisherman from Kentucky who had brought his wife and children out in their boat to do some fishing. After watching his feeble attempts to throw the net and hearing his kids whine, "let's go fishing" one too many times, I took pity on him and told him to pull up beside my boat since I had more bait fish than I needed. He was grateful.

There are clues to the best fishing spots and I was looking. Out on the ocean, you can follow the gulls that follow the bait that attract the fish. But on the backwaters and ICW where the water is calmer, you watch for schools of minnows, their little backs shining like silver while flipping in the sunlight. Fish follow their food source and they like nothing better than those little silver minnows.

I pulled up to the dock of a long abandoned seafood house on the waterway side of Holden Beach and set my anchor, hoping to find a flounder lurking around the pilings. In quick succession, I caught two Virginia Mullet and after patiently dragging my minnow back and forth on the bottom for about thirty minutes, I finally snagged a flounder, just barely the 15" regulation size. My appetite was back. I could just imagine the sight and smell of those fish, fried to a crisp golden brown, steam escaping as I pulled the snowy white flakes apart to devour them. I would cook dinner tonight and give Eleanor a break.

I pulled my boat back into the slip just as Blue Eyes was walking out on his deck, stretching and yawning. When he saw me, I swear he tightened his stomach and flexed his muscles. Not that there was too much that needed tightening. He was wearing cotton pajama pants and no shirt. There ought'a be a law....

I didn't look at his eyes and he pretended he didn't see me. I hosed down myself, the boat, and my reel, in that order; the first two to get the slimy fish stuff off, the latter to keep the saltwater from rusting my reel. I would oil it later. Then I got my cooler and tackle box out of the boat and put them on the dock. There was an old fish cleaning station built onto the dock, with a cutting board and a stainless steel sink. The stainless hadn't lived up to its name - it was rusty and pitted. I opened my tackle box and got what I needed - a lubricant to spray my reel and a filet knife to clean the fish. I spread the fish across the cutting board and made the first slice.

I felt, rather than heard a presence behind me. "The early bird gets the fish. Nice catch."

I didn't look up, just kept on cleaning my fish. "7 a.m. - best time of the day to get out on the water", I said, implying rather than saying that being in pajamas this time a day was just downright lazy.

"I went flounder gigging last night," he said. "If you and your friend want to bring those over tonight, I'll deep fry them when I cook my flounder."

"My sister." He looked at me, confused. This time I tried to look at the blue eyes instead of those gorgeous pectoral muscles that were right in my line of vision. "Uh, Eleanor is my sister, not my friend. Well, of course, she's also my friend, I guess. Yes, definitely. Eleanor is my sister and my friend."

Why the heck was I babbling? I never babble. Maybe it was because there was nowhere safe to look; those eyes, the chest.... His cheek! There's a small mole on his left cheek. I felt my confidence returning now that I had a safe place to stare.

"But anyway, that's nice of you. I'll ask Eleanor about dinner."

He reached up and brushed his cheek where I was staring.

"Good, I'll do hushpuppies and fries to go along with the fish, and you can make the coleslaw."

I guess there was no saying 'no or maybe' to Blue Eyes. "Okay. Help me clean these fish and you can go ahead and take them." We worked in silence. I gutted and scraped them while he rinsed them off. I showed off a little using my skills with a filet knife, but he didn't seem at all impressed or surprised that I could clean a fish. Stan had never cleaned a fish in his life and thought it was disgusting when I would do it. He thought it much easier to eat seafood in a restaurant. He didn't know the difference between a sea bass and a whale. And he certainly had no appreciation for fresh seafood right out of the ocean.

"See you at 6," he said as he walked off with the fish.

After he left I started feeling contrite for making the snide remark about the best time of the day for getting out on the water. He had probably been out gigging half the night.

I told Eleanor about the invitation and after resting for a while, I got up and made coleslaw while she fixed our lunch. While I was standing at the sink washing dishes, two trucks pulled into the driveway of the grey house. Blue Eyes went out to meet them and they all started carrying boxes and grocery bags inside. A little later I looked out and saw the two men drive away in one truck and leave the other behind. So this was his ride - an unassuming white Ford F-150. My estimation of the man just went up about two notches. I've never liked showy. Stan was showy, just like the cars he drove.

Eleanor and I were ringing his doorbell at 5:59.

"You're early," he said with a grin. He looked expectantly at Eleanor and I remembered that they hadn't met.

"This is my sister, Eleanor," I said. "And Eleanor, this is our neighbor Blu.., uh, Carl."

Dang, I almost said Blue Eyes.

She reached out and grabbed his hand. "Well, hello Bluh Carl," she said, laughing and highlighting my blunder.

Eleanor! For a minute there, I thought I shouted her name, but I must have just shouted it in my mind because neither of them reacted.

"I have a niece named Eleanor," he said. "It's a nice name."

He turned back to me and I once again focused on the mole. He reached up again to brush his cheek and I realized I needed to get used to looking him in the eye. He was going to get a complex about the mole, and Lord knows, I don't want to give anyone a complex. I have enough of them myself.

"Where are my manners?" he said. "Come on in. I see you've brought the coleslaw. I'll put it in the fridge and you two can go on out to the covered deck. It has a ceiling fan, so I don't think we'll be too uncomfortable out there."

As we walked through the living room on the way to the deck, I glanced around. There were several boxes on the floor waiting to be unpacked, and then I saw it leaning against the corner - a guitar. Eleanor and I both played musical instruments. She saw it too.

"Oh, look Cassie! Do you think he's any good? I wish I'd brought my violin and you, your mandolin. It would be fun to play them on the gazebo. Remember how our music sounded when we were kids, echoing across the water?"

Ha, I thought. The last thing I wanted to do was play music with Blue Eyes. There were a couple of books on the coffee table. Eleanor walked on over to the door to the deck and opened it. I stopped to read the titles of the books. They say you can tell a lot about a person from the books they read. The one on top looked interesting. Maybe I could borrow it from him. *How to Navigate the Intracoastal Waterway* - I could find my way in the dark without boat lights from Georgetown all the way down to the Georgia islands, but I had never been this far north in a boat. I picked it up and thumbed through it. I glanced at the other book as I went to put the first one back in place. *Drug Smuggling Along the Atlantic Coast.* I dropped the navigation book like a hot potato and hurried to the door to join Eleanor. Who was this guy anyway?

Eleanor was leaning over the railings looking down at the water below. I grabbed her arm and whispered, "Let's go home before he comes outside!" She jerked her arm back and looked at me like I'd sprouted alien horns.

Just then, Blue Eyes or for all I knew, Criminal Carl came bounding up the steps from below carrying a fish cooker and a gallon of oil. He looked from me to Eleanor with a puzzled expression and then shrugged his shoulders. "Let's get this Fry Daddy going," he said. He poured the oil in and adjusted the temperature control. "It'll take a few minutes to heat up. I've got the fish breaded and the bag of fries right here in the blue cooler. I've got soft drinks and a bottle of wine chilling in the red cooler. What would you like?"

To the left of the red cooler was a tall clear plastic container with drawers. I could see mugs and wine glasses in the top drawer. The other drawers held utensils, napkins and paper towels. At least he was an organized criminal. Eleanor spoke first. "I think I'll have a glass of wine, thank you, but just one."

He opened the top drawer and looked at me. "And you? What would you like? I even have some cold tea in the fridge."

Those eyes looked so twinkly and innocent. I decided to be nice and compliant for a change. You never know what these criminal types are thinking. "I'll have sweet tea, please."

He took two wine stems and a black napkin out of the drawer, then popped the cork on the wine bottle. He placed the black napkin on his left arm and poured a glass for Eleanor and one for himself. Then he went into the kitchen and came out with a glass of tea for me. When he handed me the glass, our hands touched. I would have sworn an electric current arched up in the air between our hands. He felt it too, and looked at me oddly.

"Static electricity," he said, and looked down at his shoes, then at mine. He was wearing a pair of leather deck shoes and I wore my new Cordani leather sandals that cost me a small fortune. "Ah, we both have on leather shoes and there's not much humidity in the air," he said, trying to explain away our explosive moment.

"Oh, yes," I said rather sheepishly. "Leather and low humidity - a deadly mix." But I knew full well that we were both in trouble. My chemo fried brain was now attracted to criminals and his devious mind was somehow attracted to cancer patients. I think he was getting the worst end of the stick. Whatever.

CHAPTER 5

Eleanor was enamored with Blue Eyes. She sang his praises for the next whole day.

"He's such a gentleman, Cassie. And he was so attentive to you. What do you think?"

"I guess he's good as far as neighbors go," I said. "We could have done worse."

"Why in the world did you want to leave right when we got out on his deck? That would have been so rude."

"I don't know. It was just a feeling I had." I didn't want to tell her about the drug smuggling book. I do tend to have an overactive imagination at times. "I'm glad we stayed though. He knows how to fry fish."

She smiled. "It was good seeing you have such an appetite. You ate more than I did." She paused. "Does he make you uncomfortable?"

"No, why?" It was just a small lie. I didn't know how I felt about him, really. The sparks flying were a little disconcerting. I have to admit, I was much more attracted to him than I would ever let him know.

"I don't know. You're usually more talkative to men and you actually seemed a little shy." She looked up at me suddenly. "I know! You have a crush on him."

"Eleanor, don't be foolish. I just met him, for crying out loud." I wanted to change the subject. She was getting a little too close to the truth. "The food was good though, and you're right, my appetite is improving." That would change though once chemo was started back. "When do we go to Charlotte for my scan?"

"Ten days from now. Time to fatten you up a little bit."

Simon wanted us to come to Charlotte for more scans, and the results would determine my next treatment schedule. I would probably stay with him and his wife Joan, while Eleanor and Blake visited with their daughter Liz and her family. She had married the previous summer and ten months later, their little Matthew was born.

"Cassie, you're good at changing the subject. We'll introduce our new handsome neighbor to Blake. He's a good judge of character."

***

Eleanor was right. My brother-in-law is a good judge of character and when he arrived, all seemed right with the world. Blake is the only person who has ever truly understood me. Everyone, including my father, said he robbed the cradle when he married Eleanor. She was just out of high school and he was a whopping old man of twenty-six. Robbing the cradle? Hardly - he was only eight years older than Eleanor – the same age Daddy was when he married our mama, who was just eighteen. I was twelve when they married and was going through the typical moodiness of middle child syndrome and puberty. Blake had three younger sisters and had seen it all, so he didn't just ignore me like everyone else was doing. He kidded with me and engaged me in conversation even when I didn't want to talk. He brought me out of my shell and I developed the most gosh-awful crush on him. When he realized it, he toned our conversations down, but was still very kind to me. I loved him for that and for everything he's been to our family. He always understood Simon too. Dad thought Simon should be a rough and tumble kind of guy like he was, but he was extremely bright and spent all his time soaking in new information from every book he could get his hands on. Blake encouraged him, and I'm sure he had a polite conversation with Daddy, because at some point Daddy quit ribbing his only son and seemed to be quite proud of his "book learning" as he called it. Everyone was proud when Simon became a doctor, and although I've teased him and complained, I realize how fortunate I've been to have him as my oncologist. He really is brilliant.

"Cassie, where are you?" I heard the screen door slam. It was that calm and steady voice that had helped pull me through so many rough places in my life.

"I'm in the kitchen, Blake." I called back. Although I wanted to, I didn't rush out to meet him when I saw his car pull into the driveway because I wanted to give him and Eleanor some alone time. They weren't used to being apart for so long at a time. I made my way into the living room just as he started toward the kitchen. I ran over to him and he opened his arms wide to welcome me just as he had all these years. Me, Penny and Simon, and of course Eleanor – we have all been comforted by this good man more times than any of us can remember.

He gave me a bear hug, but quickly loosened his grip as if he thought I would break. He held me at arm's length and looked me over. "We've got to get some meat on those bones," he said. He held my chin up and looked into my eyes. I saw the look of concern and he sighed.

"Are you feeling okay, Cassie? You look a little peaked." I don't know how people from the north say peaked or even if we southerners use the word properly. It means 'washed out' in our neck of the woods and we pronounce it 'peek-ed' with two syllables, and the emphasis on peek. Blake was being nice as usual. He should'a just spelled it out and said, Cassie, you look like crap.

"I feel better than I look, Blake. And your wife is trying her best to put some meat on these bones. If I keep eating like I have for the last few days...." I didn't finish the sentence because the next chemo treatment loomed over me like a cloud, but I was determined to gain as much weight as I could while I was between treatments, because frankly, I think my body would have just withered away if Simon hadn't given me a break from it.

"But you still look beautiful, Cassie. And those dancing green eyes look just as cute and mischievous as they did the first time I laid eyes on you." He stopped for a moment to think. "And how many years ago was that. Ah, thirty-seven. Do you realize Eleanor and I will be celebrating our 37th anniversary next month?"

"It doesn't seem possible," I said. That means I'm forty-nine years old. Sometimes I feel like I'm a kid again and other times, I feel like I'm sixty."

He laughed. "Well what about me? I'm sixty-four. I should be retiring soon."

"But you're a young, good looking sixty-four."

He put his arm around me and we started out the door to join Eleanor on the deck. "And you just made my day," he said.

She had pulled the grill cover off and was opening the lid. "Surprisingly clean," she said, looking up at Blake. "People usually forget about the grill when they're done cooking, and leave it for the next person to clean up."

Blake laughed. "You're talking about me, aren't you?"

"No-o-o," she said. "You would never do that!"

I loved their easy banter and had always envied them their closeness. Stan and I had just co-existed together. We were never really friends. I guess that's one of the reasons why our marriage didn't last. That, and the 'Sterile Cassie' nametag he mentally hung around my neck. It was worse than a scarlet A, and I felt the weight of it for the last five years of our marriage.

Blake looked at me. "I hope you're up to a nice juicy steak tonight. I stopped at Murray's on the way up and he iced them down for me."

Murray's Meat Market had been a landmark in North Charleston since the mid-60's and Murray Matthews was still there supervising the cuts of meat. Even though supermarkets crept in as the years went by, Murray's still had a line out the back door on the days the pork came in from the abattoir. He bought his aged beef from out West and cut it into steaks himself, always saving the tenderest cuts for his long-time customers, like Blake.

"My mouth is watering already," I said. "I can't eat a lot, though. Maybe Eleanor and I should split one."

"That's fine with me, Cassie. Blake, what do you think about us inviting our neighbor? It's only fair that we pay him back for his hospitality the other night."

"Just ask him to bring the coleslaw," I said.

"Cassie! Coleslaw was such a small thing for us to take. And he fixed a feast with the flounder he caught and even bought fresh shrimp to cook with it. We won't ask him to bring anything."

"I'm just kidding, Eleanor. Don't get so worked up."

"I think it's a good idea," Blake said. "I want to meet him anyway - just to make sure my girls are not staying beside a serial killer or something."

"Or something," I muttered. Just possibly a drug smuggler. The coast from Georgia to the Carolinas had been a hotspot for drug smuggling since the 1970's. There were a lot of arrests during those years. The temptation of easy money was more than a few shrimp boat captains could turn down. It was far easier and more lucrative to make a run a few miles out to meet South American drug runners under the guise of shrimping. The Coast Guard caught on to them by accident and a huge sting operation put local and imported smugglers out of business and in the slammer.

"You two won't need to share. I bought six steaks. I thought you might want to grill some another time."

Eleanor finished wiping down the grill. "Cassie, why don't you go over and invite him. You met him first."

"Huh-uh!" I said. "If Blake wants to check him out..." Just then Blue Eyes appeared on his deck. He looked like he was all dressed up to go out. Well, not really dressed up in the normal sense, but dressed a little nicer than beach protocol. He waved and went back in the house. I thought that was all we'd see of him for the evening, but I was wrong. He had gone out his front door and walked over the dock and up our steps. At least he's not bashful.

He strode up on the deck as if he was our long lost friend and introduced himself to Blake. "You must be Eleanor's husband. She said you were coming for the weekend."

"Yes, I'm Blake, and we were just talking about you."

Carl laughed. "That could be good or bad," he said. "If it was Eleanor talking about me, I've got a better chance." He turned around and looked at me and winked. Uh, did he really wink at me? "But if it was Cassandra, she would have convinced you by now that I'm a hit and run driver." I blushed – I'm not sure whether it was what he said or if it was the wink.

"I haven't heard about that one," Blake said, looking at me.

I shrugged my shoulders and gave Carl a piercing look. "Oh it was nothing," I said, "just a case of reckless driving."

"See, what did I tell you?" he said to Blake – rather gleefully I might add. "And just what made me the object of your conversation?" He gave me an accusatory glance. I shrugged my shoulders again and looked away. If I kept shrugging my shoulders, my neck was going to get shorter. I had never shrugged my shoulders in my life until I saw him do it a few times. He was already being a bad influence.

"Eleanor tells me you cooked a fish feast for them this week, and I wanted to return the favor. I stopped at a meat market in North Charleston on the way up and bought some great steaks. I suggested that we invite you to eat with us."

"Not Murray's?" It was more of an incredulous exclamation than a question.

"Yes, do you know about Murray's"?

"I do. Best place I've ever found to buy cuts of beef. I'm up and down the coast all the time and every time I'm through there I stock up. They have some killer sausages too."

"So you travel the coastal region quite a bit, then? What..."

"Yes, quite a bit. And yes also to your invitation to dinner. I can't turn down one of Murray's steaks. Can I fix anything?"

"Coleslaw," I said, under my breath. Eleanor gave me the evil eye with her glasses again.

"Heavens no," she said. "I make a mean salad. And we'll have baked potatoes and..." she paused. "Oh shoot! I forgot to get bread today. Blake, you'll have to make a grocery store run."

"That's one thing I have plenty of," Carl said. "And wine, I have a vintage red that I've been wanting to break open, but it's no fun to drink wine alone. After dinner, y'all can come over to my place and we'll open it." His eyes met mine - that deep blue again. "And the bread, what kind? I have garlic toast in the freezer and some sourdough. Which do you think would go best with the steaks and salad?"

"Sourdough," I chimed in. "I'm not much for garlic these days." Oops, I almost slipped. I stood there hoping Blake and Eleanor wouldn't mention my cancer. I sure didn't want any sympathy from this drug smuggler. There was something fishy about the way he cut Blake off just when he was going to ask him what kind of work he did. It was beginning to get more suspicious because he had gone out in his boat yesterday and didn't get in until the wee hours of this morning. I only knew because I couldn't sleep well. I wasn't waiting up for him or anything.

CHAPTER 6

Blake and Carl really hit it off, but that wasn't particularly surprising since my brother-in-law seems to genuinely care about people - all people. He's a good listener and never judges a person until he gets to know them...unlike me.

I wasn't obligated to make conversation during dinner except for the few questions they threw my way. It was nice to just observe. After dinner, Carl insisted on helping clean the kitchen. The tiny kitchen was close quarters for the four of us, but as Carl washed the dishes, Blake dried. Eleanor and I wiped the crumbs from the table and put the leftovers in the fridge.

"Now, to my place for wine," Carl said. He led the way with the three of us right on his heels. His house was much bigger than ours. The living room was quite large, but cozy, and a fireplace added to the coziness factor. People think of the beach as being warm in every season, but in winter, the cold air off the water can chill you to the bone. For the first time in ages, I wondered how it would be to share cold evenings, being all toasty in front of the fire, with someone I really cared about. Maybe someone with blue eyes. What was I thinking? I barely knew the guy!

The two books that were on the coffee table the last time we were there were gone and a wine tray with four glasses and a bottle of wine had taken their place. Blake and Eleanor took a seat on the loveseat right in front of the coffee table and I took a seat in one of the comfortable leather wingback chairs across from them. After popping the cork on the wine bottle and pouring each of us a glass, Carl sat in the other. The conversation was surprisingly easy and fun. I mellowed out and actually laughed when Eleanor divulged my secret penchant for being a water rat.

"She knows every nook and cranny of a fifty mile stretch of coast where we grew up. When she was ten, after begging and aggravating our daddy half to death, he finally let her go out in the boat alone one afternoon with only one stipulation. Be back before dark. Our old dog, Bones jumped in the boat with her and they were gone in a flash."

"Uh, oh, I can see where this is headed," Carl said, looking from me to Eleanor.

I smiled, and oh my gosh, it felt good to smile. He smiled back and held my eyes just a little too long. A little voice in my right ear said, "don't let your guard down, Cassie", while another little voice in my left ear said, "Go head, just relax and have fun". For once I decided to listen to my left ear as Eleanor continued her story.

"Well, dark arrived but Cassie didn't. Mama was real nonchalant about it, trying to reassure everyone that Cassie knew more about the water than most girls twice her age, and she did."

Then Blue Eyes chimed in. "But the landmarks that you know by day look so much different at night. I've seen many adults get disoriented at night out on the water."

"Exactly," I said. "I didn't know if I was going north or south."

He nodded. "Okay, I'm in suspense here, people. What happened?"

Eleanor laughed. "Well, Daddy was a good and generous man, but he was strict. Tough love back before it was called that. I begged him to go find her, but nope. He was adamant that she was going to learn the hard way. He told her to be back before dark and she disobeyed. She could just stick it out. I could just imagine her floating out in the ocean somewhere or worse, a snake or alligator jumping in her boat if she was inland. But he knew her well enough, knowing that she would hug the banks and Bones would fight to his dying breath if anything tried to hurt her."

Carl saw that our glasses were empty and poured everyone another round. When he got to mine, I stopped him at half glass and decided to sip much slower as Eleanor continued the story.

"Daddy didn't do much sitting though, more like pacing the floor. And of course, me being the oldest, I felt it was my job to pace it right along with him. Mama, Penny and Simon went on to bed without a worry in the world."

"I'm not sure I could be as tough as your father. Not now anyway. Back then, you only worried about nature's predators, not the human predators. But still... snakes, alligators." He shivered and looked at me with a new respect. "Just ten years old."

Blake tried to wander off the subject for a minute with a backwater snake story, but Carl stopped him.

"Wait, I've got to know what happened." He looked at me again. "You're here, so obviously you lived. So tell me the rest of the story." He directed his question to me.

I shrugged...again. "It's Eleanor's story. She tells it much better than I do."

"If y'all keep interrupting me, I'll never get it told."

Blake patted her on the arm. "No more interruptions, dear."

Eleanor took his hand in hers and they locked fingers. Why couldn't I have married someone who looked at me adoringly and held my hand? Stan wouldn't have done that in a million years. I loved seeing them so happy. My eyes floated over to Blue Eyes and caught him staring at me. It was disconcerting for sure, and for some reason I started wondering again; this time how it would be to lock fingers with him, but Eleanor broke the spell when she suddenly spoke.

"The next morning, right after daybreak, we heard that old Johnson motor puttering in the distance. It was the sweetest sound I've ever heard. Daddy got down on his knees, raised his arms up in the air and said, Thank you, Jesus, but he got up before Cassie rounded the corner."

"Hey, you never told me that!"

"Unh, unh, let me finish." She wagged her finger at me. "Cassie pulled up to the dock, turned the motor off and tied the boat down. Bones got off first, bounding up to the house with Cassie right on his heels."

Everybody turned and looked at me.

"It was the worst night of my life." I stopped and thought about that statement. "Well, up until that point in my life. Anyway, it turns out I was just one cove, not much more than a hundred yards from the house. I was going in the right direction all along but I didn't know that, and I was afraid I would run out of gas. From then on, I vowed never to get lost again on the water. Daddy got me a detailed map and I memorized every curve and cove and I plotted out how long it would take to get from one to the other. And Daddy started taking me out at night to get me familiar with how it looked in the dark."

"So he didn't get mad?" Carl asked.

"Oh, he was mad. My next stop after I hit the porch was the woodshed for an appointment with a hickory stick. But the best thing that came out of the whole incident was from then on, Daddy would take me out flounder gigging instead of Eleanor."

"And thank God for that!" Eleanor said. "He needed someone to help him, but I hated every minute of it. I was groomed to be more prissy, like our mama." She paused to reflect. "But mine and Mama's personalities were very different, I think."

"And thank God for *that!*"

It was Blake in one of his weaker moments, and we all busted out laughing, although Carl had no idea what we were laughing about. Our conversation was light hearted and fun, and it was as if Carl and I had an unspoken pact to keep it that way. We all told stories of our childhoods, but there was no mention of marriages, children, divorces or careers. Of course I was curious, but if he shared, I would have to share and I in no way wanted my humiliating failure at marriage or my "Big C" diagnosis to come up in the conversation. My illness was no concern of his, and the only way I could conceal it was not to get close or personal. I would just have to look away when those blue eyes locked with mine.

I started to feel a little strange, almost as if I had too much to drink, but I hadn't. A glass of wine shouldn't affect me like that, and I hadn't even finished the half glass he poured. The room seemed to be spinning around. I caught Eleanor's eye and motioned to the door. She's so attuned to my moods and frailties that she knew exactly what I wanted. She stood up and feigned a yawn, then looked at her watch. "Oh my! I didn't know it was getting so late. I don't know about y'all, but I'm exhausted." She turned to me. "You must be too, Cassie. I drug you out of bed at 6 a.m. to watch the sunrise."

I laughed and then got up from the chair. "I am pretty tired," I said. "Please let me sleep tomorrow, Eleanor. Even if the sky is on fire."

We said our thank yous and goodbyes, and it was all I could do to drag my feet across the floor. Eleanor grabbed my arm and turned on the charm. "Maybe a little more wine than you're used to? Let me help you."

Carl jumped up to come to my aid, but I pushed him away. "I'm fine, just got a little woozy there. I think I stood up too quickly." Then I willed myself to walk straight and tall on Eleanor's arm. I didn't want him to know how bad I felt. I saw his look of concern, so to throw him off, I turned to look at him when we reached the door. I even flirted a little with a coy smile. "Thanks for having us over. I had a great time."

I caught Blake looking questioningly at Eleanor and she nodded. "Oh shoot! I forgot my salad bowl."

Blake walked to the door where I stood. "Why don't I walk Cassie home and Carl can help you find your bowl."

"Sure," Carl said, leading the way to the kitchen. "There was a good bit left so I put it in the fridge so the lettuce wouldn't wilt."

When they were gone, Blake easily scooped me off my feet and carried me down the steps and back to the cottage. For once I was compliant and didn't show my independent streak. I couldn't have found that streak anywhere in my mind or body right then. My energy was zapped and I let him carry me without protesting. He carried me straight to my bedroom and plopped me down on the bed. I apologized.

"I'm sorry Blake, I hope you didn't hurt your back, but thank you! I couldn't have walked another step."

"Cassie, you don't weigh enough to hurt anybody's back. Tell me what happened back there?"

"I don't know. I was feeling fine one minute and then I just fizzled out. It was embarrassing. Do you think Carl noticed?"

"We may have thrown him off - the three of us with our telepathic signals." He laughed. "Either that or he's majorly confused right about now."

Just then Eleanor walked in the room. Her sisterly concern was thrown out the window and her nurse persona took over. "We're getting you undressed and into bed right now. And tomorrow we call the doctor."

"Oh for heaven's sake, Eleanor. You can say his name - you don't have to call him 'the doctor'. In case you've forgotten, my doctor's name is Simon."

"Okay, so we'll call Simon. You scared me, Cassie. This hasn't happened before, has it?"

"No, maybe it's a reaction to something I ate." I thought a minute. I ate a small portion of steak, a half of a baked potato, and some salad. "Or something I drank," I said, thinking about the wine.

"Maybe," she said. "Simon will know."

***

Simon's voice was scolding. "It was the wine. You can't drink alcoholic beverages with the medication you're taking for nausea. Didn't you read the warning on the bottle?"

"Heck no," I said. "I can't even read my name on the bottle. The writing's too small."

"That's why people over 40 have reading glasses, Cassandra."

Uh, oh. I hate it when he uses my whole name. He had sure heard our mother use it often enough when she was angry, and she seemed to be always angry with me. I think she was jealous that I was such a daddy's girl.

"Seriously, Cassie. Medicines by themselves can have really adverse side effects, but when you mix them with alcohol, they can be deadly. You've been taking some strong drugs lately. Please be careful."

He could be so stiff and doctorly! And I know he was thinking at the same time that I could be so stubborn and independent.

"Yes sir", I said. "I'll do what the doctor orders. Any more instructions before I hang up?"

"No, just show up for your scan next week. And Cassie?"

"Yes."

"I love you."

Dang, he must think I'm going to die. I haven't heard him say that since we were kids. "I love you too, big brother." I hung up before he could hear my voice catch. I pulled a tissue out of the box on my nightstand and wiped the tears. I know he was just being nice because he had scolded me, but I decided then and there that I'm not going to let the "Big C" beat me. I don't want to die. Since no one was in the room to call me rude, I took the tissue and blew my nose hard, making a honking sound. I was always so proud when I made that noise as a kid. Daddy would laugh and say I sounded like a goose. I miss Daddy. He didn't want to die either.

CHAPTER 7

"No, she's fine this morning. I think it was the wine. She rarely has more than a glass." I was listening from the open window of the kitchen as my brother-in-law explained my quick exit last night. The person enquiring about my well-being had a nice voice and I suddenly got goose bumps. Hoping that the goose bumps were from the chilly air this morning rather than thinking of those blue eyes, I drew closer to the window to see if I could hear more of the conversation.

"I'm glad it was nothing more serious," Carl said. "I was worried. She looked so pale." He sounded genuinely concerned and all of a sudden I could think of no wisecrack assaults to throw his way and my heart grew tender, bringing with it a wave of tears. Why was I so sensitive and emotional? I thought about checking my medications to see if my sneaky brother had put me on an antidepressant. It would be just like him to throw in a heart tenderizer among my pills! I had grown rather fond of having a hardened heart and those new raw emotions were getting the best of me.

"Why the tears?" I jumped at the sound of Eleanor's voice behind me. "I'm sorry Cassie, I didn't mean to frighten you, but I haven't seen you cry since...."

Go ahead and say it, I thought – since Stan left me. It was true. I had let those first few days after he walked out on me give way to my weaker emotions, but I had since built a thicker wall to protect my soft side.

"Tears?" I asked, rubbing hard at my eyes. "It's just my allergies. You know how I am with Fescue. We really need to get our landlord to cut this grass. The pollen's killing me."

She turned me around to face her. "It's okay to cry, Cassie. There's no one in here but me, and I've mopped up a ton of your tears when you were a kid."

I sniffed and wiped away the few remaining tears. "Yeah, every time I fell out of a tree or got in fights with those no good Harrison boys."

"I agree with the fell out of trees bit, but the Harrisons came out on the rough end of the stick when you fought them. As I recall, Joe had to have stitches after one of your punches. I'm sure glad you grew out of that tomboy stage. I felt like I should be a paid referee when you all got together."

I smiled at the thought. "Yeah, I was kicking and punching Joe one year and the next year we shared our first kiss. I wonder what happened to those boys. Their family moved away without telling a soul. One day they were there – the next day they were gone."

"You can find anybody on-line now, Cassie. There are several sites you can look. You could start with the White Pages."

"I should probably start with South Carolina's Public Records. As much trouble as those boys got into, they're more 'n likely in prison and if they are, I don't want to know about it. The memory of that first kiss would be somewhat jaded if I founded out Joe was a jailbird, don't you think?"

Eleanor laughed. "I don't know. Joe was the sweetest of the whole bunch. He might be a preacher by now."

"Ha Ha," I said. That's what I love about Eleanor. She always turns the penny over on the shiny side.

"You still haven't told me why you're crying. You're good at changing the subject."

"I have no idea why," I said. "If I did, I would stop. I hate having water faucets for eyes. I'll just blame it on the chemo like I do everything else."

"Why are my girls so serious?" Blake had walked in from the porch and was summing up our moods. "By the way, Cassie, your neighbor walked over to ask about you. He was concerned, but I just told him you were a drama queen and trying to get attention." He put his arm out in front of him, waiting for me to react. Normally I would have punched him or thrown something at him, but since I had overheard most of their conversation, I was in on the act.

"I hope you didn't tell him that you and I had planned the whole thing so we could sneak out and steal a kiss while Eleanor was in his kitchen. Oops, I just told your wife! Sorry, Eleanor." I couldn't help but laugh when he blushed three shades of red. Blake just walked away, shaking his head.

"I came in to tell you girls that I'm going out with Carl in his boat and you laugh at me." He pretended to be insulted, but then turned back around. "Think of somewhere special you want to go to dinner tonight. I think it's time to get you girls out of the house." He wagged his finger at me. "And no wine for you, Miss Drama Queen."

***

The Inlet View restaurant's name says it all. It's located on the Shallotte River inlet that dips in from the ocean between Holden Beach and Ocean Isle. The view alone is worth the trip. Carl took us by boat down the Intracoastal Waterway and pulled right up to the dock of the restaurant. The waitress seated us on the porch so we could enjoy the view along with our food. After finishing our meal, we sat sipping our iced tea and talked. Carl was easy to talk to and seemed to be enjoying being with us. Eleanor, the innocent, asked him about his personal life. Did he have children? One, he said. He had raised her with help from his mother. His wife, Rachel, had died during childbirth. I almost started crying again, thinking of how horrible that must have been for him. After his daughter, Carla graduated from college, she had married an Australian and they moved there shortly after their marriage. She just called him the week before to tell him her good news. She was pregnant, and he was already planning a trip near her due date so he could be with her. It scared him to death to think something could happen to her as it had to her mother. Eleanor, the comforter, told him the odds of that happening were slim to none and he should think positive and not convey his fear to his daughter.

He didn't speak of his job though, and when Eleanor, the curious, tried to bring it up, he changed the subject, and oddly, Blake didn't speak up or act curious at all. So much for him being our protector! A drug smuggler could be living right next door, and Blake didn't seem to have a care in the world. He seemed awfully nice for a drug smuggler, but isn't that what they do, try to blend in with the crowd?

CHAPTER 8

The weekend went by in a blur. Blake and Eleanor went to a small Methodist church down the street on Sunday morning, then Blake left for home after lunch so he could get back to work on Monday. I slept a little later than usual on Monday morning, and when I took my breakfast out to the gazebo, I noticed Carl's boat was gone. Eleanor had been wanting to go shopping to buy something for her new grandson, so I suggested we drive down to North Myrtle Beach to the outlet stores. I felt better than I had in months and we walked all over from one store to another shopping. I bought a new purse and a matching summer scarf. Eleanor is a shoe fanatic and bought three pairs. One of them matched my purse perfectly and I kept threatening to steal them when she wasn't looking. She finally agreed to let me borrow them occasionally. We found some cute things for Liz's baby. Being the great-aunt, I decided to splurge on him too.

We had lunch at the Olive Garden. The shopping trip had done us a world of good. It was good to see Eleanor happy and relaxed. Then I realized she was happy because I was feeling better. She had been so stressed out about my condition. Eleanor, always the protective big sister. I found myself morosely thinking that she would probably fall apart when I died.

We got home in the late afternoon and we both went straight to our beds and took a nap. I woke up to sounds of pots and pans in the kitchen. I walked in and Eleanor was putting the tea kettle on the burner.

"What do you want for dinner?" she asked.

"How about a bowl of cereal."

"Thank heavens!" she said. "I don't have the energy to cook. A little bowl for me. I'm still pretty stuffed from eating all that pasta."

"So am I. It was fun, just us two, going shopping. We used to do it often when we lived closer."

I got the milk from the fridge while Eleanor poured the cereal in bowls. She had finally bought some cereal I liked instead of those crunchy things she usually gets that will break your teeth off. It doesn't matter how much fiber and vitamins it has if you can't chew it. The kettle was whistling on the stovetop so I poured us a cup of hot tea and sat down.

"Yeah, we had a lot of fun together until Stan swept you off your feet and moved you to Raleigh." She looked at me. "Cassie, why didn't you move back when you divorced? I never figured you would stay away from the salt air. You love it so much."

"I really don't know. I think at first I thought Stan would grow tired of his new wifey and come back to me. Then when they started having babies, I realized it would never happen, but by that time it just seemed easier to live there than to sell the house and move. I was content with my discontentment."

She laughed. "Only you would say that. I wish you would move closer to us. You could move back in the old home place. I think all the rest of us thought you would someday. That's why we never pushed selling it."

"Peggy's daughter still lives there doesn't she? We couldn't very well throw our niece out of the house."

"Ashley's getting married in August and moving to her husband's hometown in Florida. He's a marine biologist. The house will be empty again."

I felt a pang of guilt that I had forgotten Peggy's daughter's name, much less that she was getting married. The home place - it hurt to think of selling it to strangers. All of our childhood memories are there. "I don't know. It would be a drastic move from my big house in Raleigh to the little house down there."

"You could add on, but for the life of me, I can't imagine you needing such a big house. And just think! We girls would all be close together again."

I could hear the hope in her voice and it excited me a little bit too. I really didn't have much of a life in Raleigh other than belonging to a few clubs and having lunch now and then with friends. But a writer's life is lonely no matter where you are.

"Promise me you'll think about it, Cassie. Maybe talk it over with Simon when we go up next week."

"I promise. I have been thinking about a smaller house." I wish she hadn't brought the trip to Charlotte up. It terrified me to think what the scans would show. Wouldn't it be better not to know?

"Eleanor, I'm scared."

She hopped up from her chair and knelt down beside me in mine. "So am I, Cassie. So am I." We sat there holding on to each other for several minutes, tears streaming. She finally pulled away and tore her napkin in half and gave it to me so we could both wipe away our tears. We watched a little TV together and went to bed early. I stayed awake listening and waiting for sounds of a certain blue-eyed neighbor's boat to come in. I finally fell asleep and it was still not there the next morning.

I repeated this process for the next two nights. Tuesday and Wednesday went by without a stir from next door. During the day I sat on the gazebo and wrote. Sometimes lousy moods produce good writing material and I wrote my heart out with Rafael sitting quietly on my lap.

It was almost high tide at the dock on Thursday morning when I went outside to wait. This time I wasn't fooling myself on what I was waiting on. This was the fourth day Carl had been out and I was about to file a missing person's report on him. I was beyond worried. His truck was still parked in its normal spot and hadn't been moved. I had gone over to his deck on the second night and peeked in the window. Nothing was out of place. I leaned the lid of the grill against the back door. It hadn't been moved so I knew he hadn't come in during the night and gone back out.

Last night I called Blake to see if I should report him missing. Blake was very abrupt and I was surprised.

"No, Cassie! Absolutely not! He's been on these waters most of his life. He has radio equipment on his boat and knows how to take care of himself."

"But...."

"No buts. Stay out of this. Trust me?"

Did Blake know Carl was a drug dealer or something and was trying keep me away from trouble? It made the suspicions I'd had earlier even stronger.

I watched the captain of the Lady Lu flawlessly maneuver his big boat into the narrow channel headed for the dock at Wenona's Place. Finally, something that would take my mind off waiting. One lonely gull flew over the nets and swooped down low, then flew up again, disappointed that no shrimp were in the net. He had played this game before. I looked for the old man who was usually there to meet and tie off the boats, but he was nowhere in sight. The captain pulled up close to the dock, then put it in reverse and backed up. I waited for the familiar thud of boat brushing up against the wood planks of the dock, but it didn't come. Captain Chuck was in his mid-sixties and had been on shrimp boats for nigh on fifty years. He knew how to parallel park a boat with ease. He raised his hand to his forehead in a mock salute when he saw me in the gazebo.

"G'morning," he shouted as he cut the engines.

"Good morning back atcha", I said. "Decent catch?"

"Fair to middling," he said. "Come on down. I've got something for you." I put my bare feet in my sandals and started down the steps.

I had met Chuck under the worst of circumstances the first week we arrived. I had seen the boat with the newly painted masts come in as we were eating lunch. After we had eaten, I ran inside to get my sketch pad, then walked down to the dock to check it out. The crew was nowhere around and I sat down on a wooden bench and started sketching the boat. Suddenly the toxins that had dripped through my veins a few days before raised their ugly heads. I had barely made it to the other side of the dock when I lost everything I had eaten that morning and more. I sank down on my knees with my head leaning over the side of the dock dry heaving. My energy was zapped. I heard footsteps on the dock, then felt a hand on my shoulder.

"Easy little lady," the soft voice said. "Wouldn't want you falling in."

"Right now I wouldn't care," I said.

I felt a little better and tried to lift myself into a standing position. The hand on my shoulder moved to my elbow and lifted me up. I looked up into a weathered face with kind and sympathetic eyes. He handed me a bottled water. He had already drank about half of it, but it didn't matter to me. It was good cold water and I needed it.

"Rinse your mouth out," he said. "You'll feel better."

I did as he said, leaning over the dock again, this time with his hand planted firmly under my elbow to keep me from falling.

"Thanks."

"You're welcome." He handed me a pack of gum. I took two pieces and handed the pack back to him but he wouldn't take it. "You keep it," he said. The kind eyes took in the haggard expression that I knew was on my face. I had seen it in the mirror that morning.

"Chemo?" he asked.

"Yeah, how did you know?"

"I've been there. Lung cancer. Two years ago."

"Mine's ovarian." It didn't seem at all odd to be talking calmly about my condition to a man that I had never met until just that moment. He let me hang around the dock when I wasn't barfing, and answered my million questions patiently until he left a couple of days later to go back out to sea. We were comrades in arms, bonded by the "Big C".

***

I took off for the dock. I felt like an entirely different person since the last time we met. The nausea was completely gone and I had picked up a couple of pounds.

"Take your time," he said, as he saw me running down the steps. "I'm not going anywhere. Wouldn't want you to fall and break something."

His two helpers were busy tying off and anchoring the big boat. I waved at Red. He had been on Chuck's crew for a couple of years. The other one was Johnny, a cute little guy who didn't look a day over twenty. He saluted me just as the captain had. He was the newest crew member and Chuck was proud of the way he was working out. One of Chuck's friends was a parole officer and had asked him to give Johnny a job while he was on probation. He was a good kid who had gotten mixed up with the wrong crowd. His friend was charged with kidnapping, but Johnny's role had been minor and he had ended up thwarting the kidnapper and saving the victim's life. His testimony had kept him out of prison, but he was on probation for six months.

"Whatcha got for me?" I asked impatiently.

Chuck laughed. "You're worse than a kid at Christmas," he said. He took me by the arm and helped me aboard the boat. The shrimp catch was in the large compartment at the rear of the boat where it could be easily unloaded. A smaller cooler was in the middle of the boat behind the cabin and he opened it up. It was full of fish that had been caught in the nets while trawling. He dug around and came up with two large Red Snapper.

"Oh my gosh! Are those for me?" Chuck knew from some of our previous talks that Red Snapper was my favorite fish, and we had lamented about the catch limits for the average fisherman with all the rules and regulations. It had been years since I'd had one freshly caught. "Where did you find them?"

"We're having to go out a good ways for the shrimp right now. We've hauled in about eight of the Snapper so far this year. They're finally making a comeback. As much as we all fought the fishing regulations put on the reds a few years back, it's helping to build 'em back up again. They were overfished for far too long. They're still in the 'unlawful to possess' on the recreational fisherman's rules, but commercial shrimp boats can keep our bycatch from the nets."

"Well, that makes me happy!" I said. He dropped the fish in a plastic bag and scooped some ice from the cooler on top of them.

"And whatever makes you happy tickles me to death," he said, looking down at me from his lofty six foot plus frame. "You're looking a lot better this week, Cassie. How many more treatments you got left?"

"I don't know. I go back to Charlotte next week for more scans, so it depends on what they find. If they find more cancer.... well, we'll take it one step at a time if they do."

"Johnny was talking about you today. He's been worried about you and he's got his grandma and all of her church up in Bolivia praying for you."

"That's sweet of him," I said. I didn't tell him that I had just about given up on prayer. It seemed like someone was always praying for me. First about the infertility, then the divorce, and then my cancer. Apparently God wasn't listening.

I watched as the crew took the nets down from the mast and straightened them out on the dock. They stretched them out as far as they would go; then Johnny started rolling them up as Red continued to stretch while he folded. When they had been rolled up neatly into bundles, Johnny stuffed them into canvas bags and threw them back on the boat while Red lifted up the hatch and threw them into the storage compartment.

Chuck nodded at the boys. "Get on with you boys. I know you've got your girlfriends waitin' for you."

"Not me", Johnny said sheepishly. "I haven't been off the boat long enough lately to find a girlfriend. But I'll be leaving with Red. Granny will have a hot meal warming in the oven. Pimento cheese and stale bread is getting mighty old, no offence, Captain." Chuck smiled and nodded. "Anyways, she'll have fried chicken, mashed potatoes, black-eyed peas and cornbread waiting for me."

Chuck took off his hat and combed his fingers through his hair. "You lucky dog. If I didn't have so much to do, I'd go eat some of Granny's cookin' myself. I'll call you when we get ready to set off again."

Red's girlfriend was waiting for them in her car. They took off when Johnny hopped in and Chuck turned back to face me.

"I'm putting 'er up for a few days," he said, speaking of the Lady Lu. She took on a little more water than usual this time, so I'm getting the Clark brothers to hoist 'er up and check the hull for leaks tomorrow."

"Does he have time?" I asked. "I see he's still working on Miss B."

"He'll be through with her on Sunday. He said he would squeeze me ahead of the big snowbird yacht sitting out there." He looked at the trawler perched high in the air now that it had been hoisted up using the massive rail system to get it up for repairs. He waved at the man leaning over from the roof of the cabin with a paintbrush in his hand. "It pays to have friends in high places."

I looked at the boat, too. It did seem that the man was about 100 feet up in the air.

"I wouldn't get up on that contraption for anything."

"Why not?" I asked.

"I'm scared of heights."

I guffawed. "You?"

He nodded. I thought about all the tall trees I had shimmied up when I was a kid just to get a bird's-eye view of the waterway. It had never occurred to me to be afraid of heights.

"When will you be back from Charlotte?" he asked.

"I'll be staying with my brother, who happens to be my oncologist. Eleanor and Blake are taking me up on Thursday and we'll come back here on Sunday. While I'm staying at Simon's, they'll spend a few days with their new grandson whose parents live just south of Charlotte."

"I'll be back out to sea by then. You'll be in good hands with your brother."

"I don't know. I've teased him mercilessly since he was a nerdy kid. It may be payback time."

I heard the hum of a boat engine as we talked. When you're raised around water, you get to where you recognize the little nuances of the sounds of different motors, especially those of your neighbors. Just like a dog recognizes the sound of his owner's car. Then it hit me. It was Carl's engine I was hearing.

"Oh my gosh, oh my gosh!" I said, jumping up and down.

"Whoa, slow down. You're going to fall off the dock. What is it?" Chuck looked in the direction I was looking.

"Aha," he said. The mystery man has returned."

"How did you know he was gone?"

"Gil told me he's been gone for a few days."

"I was just worried, that's all. Why wouldn't he tell someone he was going and when he would be back?"

"Someone like you?" he asked.

I blushed. "Well, me or someone else, like Eleanor. Or even Gil inside the seafood house."

He looked at me trying to figure me out. "Have you known him long?"

I shook my head.

"Well, it's my opinion he's new here and doesn't really owe anyone an explanation. I'm sure someone, somewhere knew where he was. Like maybe a wife or girlfriend."

"Oh, he's not married."

"Aha," he said.

"No, it's not like that," I stammered.

He laughed. "You protest too much. Run on and satisfy your curiosity."

"See you later," I said, and turned to walk away. I stopped and turned back. "Don't you dare say anything to him about me jumping up and down when I heard the sound of his boat engine!"

He grinned and pulled his thumb and forefinger across his lips. "My lips are zipped," he said.

I laughed and walked away. As casually as I could, I sauntered over to the other side of the dock where Carl was pulling into his slip.

"Throw me the rope and I'll tie you off," I said as nonchalantly as I could muster. He threw it and I caught it on the first try. I tied the front and he tied the back.

"Where ya' been?" I asked.

"I had some business to take care of up Wilmington way," he said, while I was tying the knot carefully. "Did you miss me?"

I looked up to find him grinning, looking very smug, in fact.

"Don't flatter yourself," I said. "I just assumed you were lost at sea, and if you weren't, you would be pulling back in here someday soon."

He laughed. "Well I missed you," he said, "and your sassy little mouth."

The way those blue eyes were lingering on my mouth, I thought I was going to swoon. Without thinking what I was doing, I licked my lips. It was an involuntary reaction.

His eyes swept back up to mine and stared intently. I thought I was going to drown in them. Before I knew it, his hand was under my chin, pulling it up to his slowly. Then his lips met mine. It was the briefest of kisses, but it made my heart beat a hundred miles an hour.

"I've been wanting to do that since the day you came storming down those steps to see if I had wrecked your boat."

I stood there frozen and couldn't think of a thing to say. He grinned at me - smug again. "Did you feed my goldfish while I was gone?"

"I didn't know you had a goldfish."

"I don't," he said, and winked. He touched my cheek again, and then turned around and walked up his steps. I watched as he picked up the grill cover that I had propped against the door. He looked from it to the grill, then back at me and shrugged. It was my turn to grin. He walked inside. Still reeling from the quick kiss, I thought about his goldfish remark. He knew he had rattled me. Chalk one up to Blue Eyes.

I looked toward the other end of the dock and saw Chuck was still there, watching me. I blushed. I think I said before, I never blush. He smiled and made the zip lips motion again. I felt more alive than I had felt in years. I feel too good to be dying, I thought. Maybe I'll make it after all.

***

"Where do you really think he's been?" I asked Eleanor as we were washing the supper dishes.

"What?"

"I mean really, shouldn't he have told us by now what kind of business he's in? I mean, he goes off in a boat and stays a few days, then comes back and stays inside most of the time. If he's on vacation like he said up front, he would be out fishing or sightseeing....or something."

"I don't think it's any of our business what he does on vacation, Cassie."

"You wouldn't," I said, a little too sarcastically.

"What's that supposed to mean?"

"It just means you're so naive. Always thinking the best of everybody. If Joe Blow out there beat up on his grandmother, you would be saying, 'Oh, poor Joe. He must have had a terrible childhood'. You're too much of a Pollyanna."

She laughed. "You're so funny, Cassie. You should have been a comedian."

"See, nobody ever takes me seriously!"

"This reminds me of conversations we used to have as kids, washing the dishes and making up the beds. You were always the curious one."

"And you were always patronizing me, just like you're doing now."

I was getting ready to throw the dish towel at her when we heard a knock at the deck-side door. The kitchen placed so that you can see just about every room in the house by taking a couple of steps. I took two steps and saw the object of our conversation standing by the screen door.

"Knock, knock," he said loudly.

"We heard you the first time," I yelled back and then got an elbow thrust into my side. "Ouch. What was that for?"

"Shush, don't be so rude." It was Eleanor in one of her bossy, big sister stare-downs. She wiped her wet hands on her apron - yes, she wears an apron - and hurried to the door. "Sorry Carl, we were just washing up the dishes. Come on in!"

"I hope I'm not interrupting," he said.

"No, not at all. As a matter of fact, I just made a fresh pot of coffee and Cassie and I were just getting ready to slice the cheesecake I made this morning. I hope you'll have some with us?" She glared at me, daring me to contradict her.

I started to say something smart just to get her back for punching me in the ribs. I actually had my mouth open to speak but I looked into those baby blues, I forgot what I was going to say. I just stood there, my mouth still open."

"Thank you, Eleanor. I don't mind if I do." he said, never taking his eyes off me. "Were you going to say something?" he asked.

"No, why."

"You had your mouth open. I thought maybe you were going to echo your sister's invitation to have cheesecake. Or were you going to tell me to go home?" He winked at me and I melted. What was it about him that made my knees turn to Jello. Maybe it was one of those bad boy, forbidden fruit kind of attractions. I needed a self-defense tactic. I squared off my shoulders, determined not to let him get the best of me.

Eleanor had already set the table with her fancy little dessert plates and was pouring coffee in the little matching teacups that held about four sips. As Carl sat down I couldn't help getting in a little dig. "Sure, I'll share. Just don't get greedy." I smiled sweetly and pulled out the chair on the opposite side of the table.

"Cassie!" Eleanor stopped in mid-stride and looked at me in disbelief, then turned toward Carl. "Carl, I apologize for my sister's rude behavior. I don't know what's got into her."

He stared at me with a smile of his own, never taking his eyes off my face. It was sort of unnerving. "I don't know," he said. He paused as though he was assessing me. "She's sort of cute when she's protecting her food. Sort of like a cat I once had."

A cat - he was comparing me to a cat! And cute! Did he just call my forty-nine year old self cute? He was making fun of me.

Eleanor looked confused as she looked from me to Carl and then just shook her head. "Whatever. I'm taking my cheesecake to the bedroom to call Blake. I'll leave you two to your own craziness. If I hear dishes being thrown, I'll come out and referee. Just don't break Grandmother Bella's good china. She'll come back and haunt me."

The image of our grandmother flying over the dining room to haunt Eleanor made me laugh. "That would be just like her," I said.

"Don't worry, we'll try to be civil," Carl said, and dug into his cheesecake with gusto. It was obvious he was enjoying every bite he put in his mouth. He looked to see me watching him. "Oops, sorry," he said. "I'm inhaling it. It's been awhile since I've had homemade desserts."

He looked like a little boy, and my heart softened. "Eat all you want," I said. "I was just kidding."

He put his elbow on the table and reached across the table with his pinky finger in the air. "Truce?" He asked, smiling.

I interlocked mine with his. When our hands touched, sparks flew, just like they'd done before.

He looked down at his shoes. "Flip-flops," he said, and looked up. "I'm beginning to think there's more to this than static electricity."

I smiled. "Truce," I said. We stared into each other's eyes and held our interlocking pinky fingers together much longer than necessary to call a truce.

CHAPTER 9

The big trawler came into view and pulled up beside the Lady Lu. A dirty looking man who looked as if he hadn't bathed since 1984 stuck his bearded face out of the open window of the cabin and let out a stream of obscenities first, then followed up with, "You takin' up enough room for two trawlers, Charlie boy. Why don't you learn how to dock one of these things?"

I looked at Chuck's boat. There was about 3 feet between his boat and the one behind it. Perfect parking if you ask me. "Who is that", I said with disgust. "Somebody needs to wash his mouth out with soap."

Chuck laughed. "He could stand to use a few bars of soap on the rest of him, too." He wrinkled up his nose. "Nobody can get downwind of him without gagging."

The name written on the boat was Black Jack. "I thought there was some sort of unspoken rule to name the trawlers after a lady," I said.

"I don't think Jack knows any ladies well enough to name a boat after one." He said. "By the way, stay away from him. I've heard too many stories."

"Don't worry about that. One look at him is enough to convince me."

"He doesn't dock here often," he said. "He usually pulls in up at Southport." He turned to look at me. "I wouldn't want him knowin' that you and Eleanor are staying in the house by yourselves." He watched as the trawler took a circle and headed for the dock right in front of the Lady Lu.

"Dang it. I was hoping he would harass all of us and then move on down to Gray's Landing. He usually sells his shrimp to them when he has any. Gil doesn't like to deal with him here."

"Maybe he didn't have a good catch", I said.

"That's likely. It's sort of strange that he's out there longer than any of the rest of us and comes in empty handed about half the time."

Chuck was pacing about on the dock. It was the first time I had ever seen him ruffled. He's usually so calm and cool.

"Go on, Cassie. I don't want you around when he gets off his boat. Walk down the dock to the boat landing and take those stairs. Then pretend you're going anywhere but to your house."

"You're scaring me," I said.

"I just don't trust him. I've seen him around women before and there's no telling what will come out of his mouth. Go on, skedaddle."

I did as he said. I took the steps down from the boat landing and walked up the road a bit. On my way back, Carl pulled his truck up beside me. "Want a ride?" he asked.

I hopped in. The back seat was filled with grocery bags. We pulled up to his front door and I helped him unload his groceries. He pulled two bottled waters out of the fridge and we sat down at his kitchen table. He set the bottle of water in front of me.

"You look like you could use a cold drink," he said. "What were you doing walking up the road in this heat? My truck thermometer was registering ninety-eight degrees."

I did feel hot and sweaty. "Captain Chuck made me do it," I said. He looked at me incredulously.

"What? He made you walk on the road?" Then he realized I was kidding and smiled. "I thought most ship captains made people walk the plank."

"He doesn't have a plank so he uses the road. No, seriously, he wanted me out of there because this dirty old trawler came in. The Black Jack."

He almost choked on his water and stood up, knocking the chair over as he stood. "What? Jack Crum is docked here?"

"Uh, I didn't get his last name. Chuck was too busy shooing me away."

"Good for Chuck. I'll walk you home, by the front way, not on the dock-side. Then I've got to come back here and make some phone calls."

"So you're shooing me away too. I'm beginning to feel unwanted." I did my best to make a pouty mouth, but I'm not good at flirting. He laughed at me. I pushed myself away from the table and stood up. Before I knew what was happening, he was right beside me. I turned to see what he was doing and he put both hands on my shoulders and held me at arm's length. I was hoping for another kiss, a little more lingering this time, and I set my mouth for one and closed my eyes. It never came and I opened my eyes, embarrassed. His expression was sweet and sultry all at the same time. Then he looked into my eyes.

"I don't want to shoo you away. I wish...." He cut himself off and took a deep breath. "Never mind what I wish, just mind what Chuck said, Cassie. Jack Crum is a no good scumbag."

I very much minded what he wished as he walked me to the front porch of our house. "Thanks for giving me a lift," I said, as I opened the screen door. My sweaty hair was dry now, but was hanging in little ringlets around my face. One was hanging down over my left eye and he reached up and brushed it back off my forehead.

"Cassie, please keep your doors locked until this guy leaves. Promise?"

I nodded my head, hoping for another touch, but he turned on his heels and left without saying another word.

CHAPTER 10

Carl

It was hard keeping up the guise of a vacationing fisherman, but day after day, I would guide my boat out to the spot where a cargo ship was expected to show up, but day after day I was disappointed. I would catch a few fish and throw them in my cooler, but I threw back more than I caught. I didn't want to go over the limit and attract the attention of the local game wardens as I made my way back in.

To throw off any suspicion, I always cleaned my fish in full view right on the dock. Cassie was the only one who didn't seem to trust me, but I had a feeling she'd been hurt before and was suspicious of men in general. Except for Captain Chuck and her brother-in-law, Blake; she seemed at ease with them. I liked Blake, and for some reason he trusted me, but he made it clear that if anyone hurt his girls, there would be trouble. When he told me he was an engineer at the Savannah Nuclear Power plant, I had a feeling he would be searching for Carl McGee on the internet. I knew he would find that Carl McGee lives a nice clean life as a contractor in the Wilmington area.

I couldn't get my mind off the little green-eyed minx and I knew if anyone would get hurt in all this, it would be me.

I could tell by looking in her eyes she'd been hurt before, and I wondered if it was a new hurt or an old one, and was she in a relationship or not. I should have minded my own business and not made any contact with my neighbors at all, but my blasted boat bumping into hers started the roller coaster uphill battle of our rocky relationship. Despite my intention of being careful, I knew there was something about her that could do me in. Funny, witty, way too thin, but hauntingly beautiful.

I wondered if she thought about me at all. Was she even remotely attracted to me? She didn't break away when I kissed her, but then again, I didn't give her much time to. And Lord have mercy, why did I kiss her anyway? I've never done anything so spontaneous in my life. I just couldn't help myself. Those defiant eyes couldn't mask the gentleness I saw underneath the surface, and when she licked her lips, my resolve slipped away. One thing for sure, being around her made sparks fly.

I decided to make one more run to scout around for the ship. My motor cranked right up and I gunned it. The ocean was as calm as a lake, so in no time, I was back at the coordinates on my GPS. I was almost there when I saw a shrimp trawler in the distance. Without even getting close enough to see the name, I knew it was the Black Jack. This is not an area that normal trawlers pull their nets. What's he up to, I wondered? Maybe looking for the same ship. I followed him at a safe distance for some time, but then another trawler came in sight. I couldn't make out the name. It seemed to be heading in the same direction we were going, but then veered off course. Did he see Jack and change directions to avoid him?

CHAPTER 11

For three days in a row, Carl went out early in the mornings and returned late in the afternoon, seemingly to avoid me. I can't say that I blamed him since I was sarcastic one minute and practically begging for him to kiss me the next. I had gone completely bonkers, so it was sort of a relief not to have to deal with him.

I took my boat out for a while. It was a good day to go fishing. The ocean was flat and all the talk at the boat landing was that the black bass were biting at the shipwreck reef. I had snacks and plenty of water in the boat. I always carry enough water to get me by for a week because in my opinion, people who perish at sea are crazy for not taking enough water in the first place. A couple extra gallons of water isn't going to sink a boat. You can catch your own food if you're resourceful. Everybody knows that raw fish is just sushi without the big price tag and without all the little fillers rolled up inside. I don't like raw fish, but I could live on it a few days as long as I have my little mini-packs of M&M's to wash it down. I double checked on the M&M's. Yep, they were there.

I figured puttering out to the reef would take my mind off of my upcoming trip to Charlotte. Eleanor and I were taking a picnic lunch the next day across the waterway to the deserted east end of Holden Beach. It's not totally deserted but only the people who make a real effort by going there by boat or walking a half mile through soft sand can reach it. We were going by boat.

It's beautiful, and if you get there early before the people drift in, you can imagine it like it was since the beginning of time - all sand dunes, sea oats and white beaches meeting the water's edge.

The sea wasn't resisting my little boat at all as I glided effortlessly through the water. It can turn on you in an instant though; one minute a glass lake, the next a raging tidal wave. You just have to watch the sky for clouds that can turn into a squall, and get the heck out of Dodge before it happens.

It was relaxing going at my own pace. The dolphins were loving the smooth surface and were swimming alongside me, when suddenly one plunged his entire body out of the water just inches away and splashed a fine spray right in my face. The others seemed to be laughing at me and I laughed right along with them. It was glorious - just me and those sleek black creatures with the intelligent eyes! It was if they could read my mind and knew that I needed cheering up.

Weighing heavily on my mind was the chemo treatment I would have to have after the scan. And even worse, the blasted shot the next day to boost my immune system. The chemo was bad, but the Neulasta shot made every bone in my body ache for a solid week. I thought I had come down with the flu the first time I had one, but Simon said it was a common side effect of the shot. I was dreading it. I was finally feeling good. I owed it all to Eleanor because of her force feeding me and watching over me like a mother hen. I was grateful she stepped in to prevent me from going it alone, like I had stubbornly done the other times.

I didn't dare hope that he would skip the shot, because every hope I've had in the last fifteen years has been dashed. Sometimes I feel like I'm wearing an albatross around my neck. Granted, they're supposed to be bad luck on a boat, but when you have one dangling on a chain, you feel you've been shipwrecked. Poor me! I was beginning to sound like a broken record.

Speaking of shipwrecks, the reef was just ahead, and I could only see one boat. My luck was changing; it moved out. There was nothing else in sight but a shrimp boat in the distance and the smaller boat seemed to be following it. It looked a lot like Blue Eyes' boat. Too bad I didn't bring my binoculars, but at least I could do a little fishing.

Right at dusk, he finally pulled his boat up to the dock. He couldn't see me because I was sitting in one of the short chairs, peeking through the slats of the gazebo wall.

As I watched, he tied the boat off and pulled his cooler out of the boat onto the dock. Then he sat down on the dock bench with a defeated look and put his phone up to his ear. The quiet of the evening caused his voice to waft up in the air and I could hear him just as if he were sitting in the gazebo with me. I wasn't really eavesdropping, just sitting there minding my own business, but it's frustrating when you can only hear one side of a phone conversation.

"Yep, I found it. It's a cargo ship - not too big. Not far from where our source said it would be. I kept my distance though and nobody saw me."

"What? No, I couldn't get through. There was no reception and I didn't want to risk using the radio since it doesn't have a secure frequency."

"Yea, I know. I got a pretty good look with my binoculars and there are all kinds of antennas. Could you have Doc bring me one of the new radios tomorrow and the program instructions?"

"Great, what time? I'll be here. And by the way, guess who else is on the scene around here?"

"No, not Osborne. It's Jack Crum. I think he could be involved too."

"I don't have any real evidence, but it's likely."

"I'll be careful. Just get that radio to me and if I need any help, I'll call you."

"Ha ha, I'm not that stupid. I can probably get close enough, but they may be heavily guarded with all the drugs on board so I won't try anything without you."

"What's that? You still think we should handle it that way? I'm not so sure. I don't think they'll take kindly to a fishing boat just pullin' up to their side. Let's scratch that and stick to the original plan. It's risky, but we've got to do what we came to do."

"Yeah, I don't think it'll be long. I have one complication though."

"Never mind, I can handle it. I'll talk to you tomorrow. Okay, see ya."

I watched as he put his phone back in his pocket and sat there with his head between his hands. "Yep," he said so softly I had to strain my ears to hear him. "A complication indeed. One of the worst kinds." He lifted his head and gazed up at the stars. "A complication of the heart."

I wondered what he meant by that, but I was too busy worrying about his conversation to dwell on it. Was he referring to a drug ship? Was he and another friend planning to sneak up to it and steal drugs from it? That would make them criminals stealing from other criminals and nothing good could come from that. Plus he might get shot. All of a sudden, I was frightened. Surely, I misunderstood the conversation. I reached into my pocket and pulled out my lucky rabbit's foot. "He can't be a criminal, he can't be a criminal", I whispered. Maybe if I repeated it enough times....

Just then, the screen door opened and closed loudly and Eleanor came out on the deck. I slipped out of my hiding place in the gazebo and joined her as if I had just walked out with her. She started to speak, but I put my finger up to my lips. "Shh", I whispered.

Carl looked up. "Good evening, ladies. Nice weather we're having tonight, isn't it?"

"A little too warm inside," Eleanor said. "Thought I would come out here and catch the breeze."

"It's been hot and sticky on the boat too." He looked up at us and smiled, and what a smile. All my doubts about him melted away. "I've got an idea," he said. "I'll take the cooler inside and take a quick shower and then take you two down to the Beach Shack to get some ice cream."

I was hoping Eleanor would say yes. Maybe I could drill him with some innocent conversation.

"I'm afraid I'm going to have to pass," she said. "I'm expecting a call from Blake. We have to firm up our plans about going to Charlotte on Thursday." She looked at me. "But Cassie, why don't you go with him? You need to get out of the house for a while."

"How about it, Cassie?" Carl asked. "They have the best chocolate ice cream I've ever had."

Eleanor walked back inside. "Sure," I said. "I'll get a sweater in case it's windy on the beach side."

"Great, I'll knock on the front door when I'm ready..." He paused for a second, then I could hear the humor in his voice and see it in his eyes as the soft glow of the dock light beamed down on his face. "Just like a real date."

I was thankful that the light was shining on the dock below and that I was relatively in the dark. I wouldn't want him to see me blush like a schoolgirl!

The front seat of his truck was cluttered with papers. He gathered them up quickly but an envelope fell to the floor and I got a good look at it as he was putting the rest of the papers in the back seat. It was from the power company and addressed to someone named William C. Wright. One of his friends who delivered Carl's truck to him must have accidentally left his mail in it. I still didn't know what to think about the conversation I had overheard. I wanted Carl to be a good person. He seemed like a good person; but good people can be tempted by all kinds of things and can end up being a rotten apple in a skinny minute.

My ex came to mind. His rotten apple moment happened when he strayed from our marriage. It didn't make him a bad person, per se, but it was wrong - just plain wrong, and it hurt like the dickens. But, it isn't illegal to have an affair and it's a major crime to be involved in drugs.

Just when I find a man I'm attracted to, he turns out to be a felonious criminal! It wasn't a good thought. What the heck? What harm could it do to just go out and have a good time? It could be my last opportunity since criminals do eventually get caught. Hmm, rational thinking has never been one of my strong points.

Tucked underneath the bridge that rises high over the waterway connecting the mainland to the island is an unassuming little ice cream shop called the Beach Shack. It's one of those so-called creameries where they put the ice cream on a marble slab and slap it around adding whatever ingredients you choose. They slapped ours around for nothing since all we wanted was plain chocolate. The teenaged boy with spiky blonde hair and a nose ring kept asking us the whole time he was slapping our ice cream if we were sure we didn't want chocolate bits, sprinkles or coconut flakes added. It must have been a slow night for business in the Beach Shack.

I looked at the clock on the wall. 9:50 p.m. They closed in ten minutes. Maybe he was trying to meet his quota for ice cream accessories if there is such a thing.

Since we didn't want to be run out at closing time, we took our cones outside to one of the cafe tables. Mistake. The heat and humidity combined was making the ice cream melt faster than we could eat it which made us lick it furiously as we tried to stay one step ahead of each drip.

"You look just like a kid trying to gobble it down before someone takes it away from you," he said, laughing as he watched me bend over, finally giving up the battle and letting it drip between my feet.

I corrected him. "I may act like a kid, but I sure don't look like one. I lost my youthful glow a long time ago." I laughed and pointed at his shirt and then at mine. "You too! We're definitely as messy as a couple of kids."

His blue eyes reached out and grabbed mine. I swear, they did. It's like both our eyes are magnets and they lock in on each other.

"You sell yourself short, Cassie. There are different stages of youthful glow. Maybe that skinny teenage boy in there wouldn't think so, but to me, you've still got it."

Flattery will get you everywhere, I thought, and I smiled at the way he expressed himself. Did I still have it? No, I don't think I ever had it in the first place. I wanted to mock him, but at the moment, with the stars aligned just so, the bridge over the waterway making a frame for the newly risen moon and being lost in a pair of blue eyes, I couldn't think of a single sarcastic comeback.

"How old are you, Cassie?"

To some women my age, that would sound like an extremely personal question, but I am what I am and I've never minded telling my age. "I turned forty-nine last month", I said.

"Aha, an older woman!" His eyes were teasing.

Rats, I was afraid of that. He's probably forty-two or something. My face fell.

"I don't turn forty-nine until next month. You're a whoppin' two months older than me."

Why was I relieved? I let out a long sigh, then smiled. "You know what they say about older women, don't you?" I had no idea what they say about older women or why that came out of my mouth.

As if he knew I was just making nervous chatter, he laughed. "No, you'll have to tell me sometime but right now, let's throw this messy cone away and walk on the beach." He grabbed my hand and pulled me from the bench.

What could I do? I was being carried away against my will and I hurried as fast as I could to keep up.

CHAPTER 12

The public beach access walkways are built over the dunes to protect the fragile eco-system of sea oats and sand. We climbed the stairs easily going up the walkway, but they're steep leading down to the beach. The last step was a doozy. It appeared that the last high tide carried a good layer of sand from underneath it. Carl stepped down before me and took my hand. He put his other arm around my waist and swung me from the stairway into the sand. It happened so fast that my independent side didn't have time to react or object even if I'd wanted it to. The momentum of his move knocked him off balance and we both almost fell.

"Whoa!", he said, laughing. "You're even lighter than I thought." He held me in his arm for a few more seconds to get our balance. The moon highlighted the blue of his eyes as we stood facing each other. Without a word, he turned me loose, but didn't let go of my hand as we started walking and I made no move to take it away.

What was I doing walking hand-in-hand with a man on the beach that I barely knew and feeling that it was the absolutely normal thing to do? Right then, right there, it didn't matter to me if Carl was a drug smuggler or a Catholic priest. I was purely smitten. There was a little bell ringing in the far corner of my left brain that I should have taken as a warning sign, but when has Cassandra Phillips ever listened to little bells?

We walked in silence for a while. Our strides matched but I could tell he was holding back so I could keep up.

My stamina was zilch, zero, and not far into the walk, I stopped. His hold on my right hand made him come to an abrupt stop which jerked him around to face me.

"I need to rest for a minute", I said. "I have a stitch in my side." It was a small lie but not much of one and I laughed to myself at the irony of it. There had been a full row of stitches at my surgery incision running from one side to the other; my bikini line, they called it. But they were healing. The little marks from the staples they used to stitch me back together were still red and tender, but it was the lack of energy that held me back, and Carl had no way of knowing that. The time had not yet been right for me to share my cancer diagnosis and treatment with him. So far we had only shared small talk, and as much as I wanted to be able to share my thoughts and feelings with him, my suspicions just wouldn't go away.

"I'm sorry," he said. "My legs are longer - I should have thought about that. Let's find a place to sit. Look, there's a walkway. We can sit on the steps."

Why does he have to be so nice? Of course, even Bonnie and Clyde were nice at times.

The steps belonged to one of the beach houses that lined the ocean front. The occupants could step out of their house, follow the walkway over the dunes and be on the beach in a matter of a couple of minutes. There were lights on in the large room facing the beach but there was no sign of anyone about.

"Do you think they'll mind if we sit here?" I asked.

"They probably won't even know we're here," he said, "and if they do and don't want us here, I'm sure they'll tell us." He turned loose of my hand, and pointed to the sky over the ocean. "Wow, look at that moon!"

I looked and felt at ease sitting by his side. He linked arms with me.

"It's a Carolina moon," he said.

I laughed. "North or South Carolina? They're different, you know."

"How so?"

"Maybe not so much anymore. The Lowcountry moons of my growing up years were magnificent. We were in a secluded cove with no lights at night other than the soft glow of the yellow porchlight. The light of the moon, especially full moons, would illuminate our perfect little world, right there on the water. The marsh grasses turn golden, just as they do in the sun. You can even see your shadow fall upon the water. On cold winter nights, there's an eerily luminescent glow that seems magical somehow. I wish I could describe it. You just have to be there."

"You've done a good job of describing it. Is the house where you grew up still standing?"

"It is, and Eleanor's trying to convince me to move back."

"What's stopping you?"

"Too many things, right now. Maybe later." He didn't ask any more questions and I didn't offer any more information. Maybe I would go back someday. I could see his profile clearly as he gazed out over the ocean. I realized just how little I knew about him. He was handsome; he had fabulous eyes; and he seemed kind, but what was he hiding? There had been no mention of what he did for a living. Had I asked? No, not really, just the subtle change of subject when he's the focus of a conversation. As if feeling my eyes boring into him, he turned around and looked at me.

"Penny for your thoughts?" he said. He had turned back to me while I was caught up into my own thoughts.

"Do you really want to know?" I asked. Before he could say no, I went on. "I was just thinking that I don't know anything about this guy I'm walking on the beach with. He could be a serial killer for all I know."

"Moi?" He smiled. "A serial killer? Surely you don't think that?"

"Well, maybe not. But I don't even know what you do for a living. And you act so mysterious."

He laughed. "What I do isn't all that important. Trust me. As a matter of fact, I'm taking time this summer to decide if I want to change jobs. I'll let you know by the end of the summer."

"Is that all you're going to tell me?"

"For now." He looked uncomfortable. "Just trust me, okay?"

"I suppose. I probably won't see you after the summer anyway, so why should it matter?" I felt a little weepy at the thought.

I looked up at the moon again. It had risen higher over the ocean and had the illusion of a halo surrounding it. "Look," I said. "It's not a Carolina moon after all. It's a melancholy moon."

"And what's a melancholy moon?"

"Ever heard of the Andrews Sisters?"

"I think they were before my time."

"Mine too, but I grew up listening to my mom singing one of their songs. And her singing it stands out vividly in my personal bank of memories. She gave up a wealthy lifestyle to marry my dad. She was used to an active social life. When she married Daddy, he took her out in the sticks, or I should say out in the marsh, to live. Except for church and an occasional Lowcountry Boil given by other backwoodsy neighbors, there was no social life at all. It was a way of life that was beneath her class. I don't think she was ever truly happy living there. She had a beautiful voice and I would hear her outside at night singing this song called *Melancholy Moon* by the Andrews Sisters on clear nights."

"Do you know the words?"

I laughed. "Yeah, they've been stuck in my head for years. Eleanor's too. Sometimes it brought tears to my eyes when she sang it."

"I'd like to hear it."

I hummed to get on the right key. "I'll just sing the last verse so you can get the gist of it." I started singing."

"The world without you is a world that's out of tune.

It's a sorry serenade to a mighty lonely me and a melancholy moon.

Make it soon, here we'll be, a mighty lonely me and a melancholy moon."

"Wow. You must have inherited that voice from your mother." He reached for my hand and held it. "Do you think your mother regretted her decision to marry your father?"

"I don't know that she regretted it. It was more like she questioned her decision and wondered how things would have turned out had she stayed in Charleston. She spent so many years pining away for what she lost by coming to such a secluded place, that she didn't enjoy life as she should. What we had was far more beautiful than the memories she had of Charleston, but I don't think she ever saw it as I did. She was lonely." A lot like me, I thought.

"You don't have to be lonely, Cassie." Where did that come from? It was as if he could read my mind. "I would love to spend more time with you. Maybe someday you'll learn to trust me."

I just kept looking at the moon, a stray tear or two sneaking out from my eyes.

"It's not my song," I said. "It's my mother's." Who was I kidding? Had I become so much like Mama? Speaking the words to Carl brought a sudden revelation that I was living her life all over again. Pining away for a husband that I couldn't hold onto, and holding the bitterness in my heart, had kept me from enjoying what could have been the best years of my life.

He didn't say anything, but continued to hold my hand. After a while, he stood up and pulled me up beside him. "Come on, let's get you back home before your sister starts worrying about you."

"She won't worry. I can take care of myself." At the moment I didn't feel like I could take care of myself. I felt lost in his eyes.

"Don't you like someone else taking care of you now and then?" he asked. "Like me?" He didn't wait for an answer and I didn't pull back when he leaned in to kiss me. "Like this?" he murmured, pulling me in closer.

"No, like this." I said, kissing him back with a passion that I didn't know still lived inside my soul. The kiss brought the realization that life's too short to worry about what a person does for a living. I would wait until the end of the summer. If he wasn't in jail by then, maybe there was hope.

"Whoa," he said, when I finally broke away. "That's exactly what I meant."

We drove the short distance back from the beach in his truck in companionable silence. When he stopped the truck, he made no move to get out, but turned to face me.

"Tell me about your trip to Charlotte on Thursday."

I looked away from him. "I'll be staying with my brother and his family for a few days while Eleanor and Blake go to visit their new grandson just a few miles south of Charlotte."

"What does your brother in Charlotte do?"

I shifted uncomfortably, but he didn't seem to notice. "He's a doctor. He was the brainy one."

"See, I don't know much about you either. What do you do for a living? I assume you live alone in Raleigh?"

"I've lived alone since my divorce. And I write novels for a living. Well, not much of a living, but I do okay." I didn't tell him about my alimony check from Stan each month. If he could keep secrets, so could I.

"I sense there's something you're not telling me," he said.

I grinned. "If you're not in jail by the end of the summer, I'll spill the beans," I said.

He laughed. "Fair enough." He reached over and kissed me lightly on the lips. "I'll be here."

I started to open the door, but he stopped me. "No, let me do it."

I waited patiently until he came around and opened the door. He grabbed my sweater out of the back seat and put it around my shoulders. I put both hands behind my neck and flipped my hair out from under the sweater. He was standing so close.

"Good night, Cassie." His breath was warm on the back of my neck. I turned around to face him. "I'm running the boat up to Wilmington tomorrow so I won't see you. If I'm not back by the time you leave Thursday, I hope you have a good trip."

Rats! I don't know why it mattered, but knowing I wouldn't see him for almost a week was depressing. But there was no way I was going to let him know that. "Okay, I'll see you next week," I said. "Thanks for the ice cream and the walk on the beach."

I started to walk away, but he caught my arm and turned me around to face him. "It was my pleasure," he said, looking at me with a glint of humor in his eyes. "Especially the kiss."

I smiled and broke free. "Good night, Blue Eyes," I said, walking away.

"You noticed."

"Yeah," I said, pulling my sweater tighter around my shoulders as a shiver went down my spine. I kept walking. The night air was chilly, but the blue eyes I was thinking about made me feel warm, very warm.

I stopped and glanced back. He was still standing there. I waved and he waved back, then I watched him walk inside the grey house from the shadows of the large pecan tree that stood beside our deck. I glanced out at the shrimp boats floating majestically in a row lining the docks. The masts of the boats looked as if they were pointing straight up to the moon. The Lady Lu was perched patiently upon the track lift, waiting her turn to be repaired. The Lucky Linda and Sweet Sue's decks shone brightly in the glow of the moon, but docked beside them was the ominously dark hull of a boat, the Black Jack. As I watched, I saw a movement on the lower deck of the ship. I could just make out the outline of a person - creepy. I slipped out of the shadow and ran inside the house, double locking the door behind me. This time when I shivered, I felt cold, very cold.

Carl

It was true. I had been thinking of changing professions, and sitting under the full moon with Cassie beside me drove the point home. It was a feeling I'd been having recently, needing to find something less stressful and safer. Things were getting too dangerous, especially with Jack Crum around. Besides, it's hard to have a romantic relationship when you're afraid of putting someone else in danger. There had only been two women that I'd cared for since Rachel passed away, and they didn't stand the test of time. But this was different. A magnetic force seemed to be pulling me into a relationship with Cassie whether I wanted it or not. I wanted to believe the same was true with her. She seemed so stand-offish at first, but I had discovered beneath the surface a beautiful woman who had been hurt. I've always been a sucker for a damsel in distress. But how could I protect her when I was living on the edge myself?

But now to focus on getting close to the freighter. Doc would be by in the morning. Two heads are better than one.

CHAPTER 13

On Thursday morning, Eleanor, Blake and I had breakfast at the table before our trip to Charlotte. We sat in silence, each of us absorbed in our own thoughts and dreading the day ahead of us. I had gone to bed early the night before, but sleep had eluded me. At 2 a.m., I finally got up and made a cup of coffee and took it out on the deck. The Lady Lu's repairs had been completed on Wednesday and as I sat there sipping my coffee, I was surprised to see she had left the dock sometime during the night. I hadn't heard her leave. Crum's boat was still docked where it had been for the last few days. He must have been staying on his boat, because I hadn't seen hide nor hair of him. After I finished my coffee, I went back inside and was finally able to sleep until my alarm sounded at 6 a.m.

Surprisingly, the Lady Lu was back at the dock this morning, looking as if she never left. Maybe I was dreaming she was gone, or maybe Chuck had engine trouble and came back in. Carl had left the morning after our walk on the beach, just as he had said, on one of his secret missions. Maybe he was FBI or something. That would sure be better than being a drug smuggler.

At 7:30, Eleanor and I walked out the front door. Blake was already in the car waiting for us. I glanced at the grey house. Eleanor was watching me.

"It's dark over there", she said. Where did Carl go off to?"

"I thought you knew. He mentioned he would be gone a few days. He left Tuesday."

She looked at me sideways. "He's somewhat of a mystery, isn't he?"

"Mysterious is an understatement," I said, somewhat sarcastically.

"You're pouting! Is our neighbor the reason you've been moping around the house since yesterday?"

"Me, moping?" I tried to look indignant, but I didn't pull it off.

"It is! I think you have a crush on our neighbor."

"Really, Eleanor. You're just now noticing this? Why, he practically proposed to me under the full moon at the beach the other night."

She stopped dead in her tracks and looked at me with her mouth wide open. I laughed at her shocked expression. "Honestly, Eleanor, you can be so gullible. I'm just curious about him, same as you. You're the one who asked me where he's gone off to."

***

The scenery along Highway 74 from Wilmington to Charlotte is unchanging and mostly bypasses the small towns until you get to the last leg of the trip. I was enjoying hearing Blake and Eleanor talk about little Matthew, their grandson. But I was curious about Liz's marriage. I hadn't heard the full story.

"So tell me the details, Eleanor. How did Liz meet this new man after Ron died?"

"Haven't I told you this before? You came to the wedding."

"And you and I have also been together day and night for about a month now, but the subject's never come up and I forgot to ask. Humor me."

"It's a complicated story and takes a long time to tell, which is probably why we haven't talked about it before."

"Wait up," I said. "Let me change seats so I can hear you." Blake was driving, so I moved on his side of the car where Eleanor wouldn't have to strain her neck to talk to me.

"That's better," she said. "Did you ever visit Liz and Ron in Park Place."

"No, I'm afraid I've been a hermit for too many years. I should have, but just never got around to it. The last time I saw Ron was at Dad's funeral. He died just a year or two after Dad, didn't he?"

"Yes, and his funeral was in his old hometown in Georgia where his parents still live. He had just turned forty-one when he died of what's called a Widowmaker heart attack."

"Poor Liz. She must have been devastated?"

"She was. And Cassie, I thought about you during her time of grief, and it made me realize even more the grief you felt when Stan left you. It seems just as bad or worse when someone you love divorces you. At least Liz knows that Ron wouldn't have left her if he could have possibly stayed."

"I hadn't thought of it that way," I said. "I did feel grief, just as if I had lost him completely, but at least I could tell him how I felt. Liz didn't have that." Neither of us said anything for a moment, lost in our own thoughts.

"But, you know, somewhere along the way I stopped feeling the pain. I finally saw that we both would have been miserable if we had stayed together. He wanted babies and I felt guilty that I couldn't have any. And if he hadn't left when he did, he probably would have left when I got sick, because he couldn't handle anyone being sick. He almost never went to visit his parents when they were sick. He would have never visited if he hadn't been worried his dad would leave everything to the church. Lord, he threatened to often enough. It would have served him right. But back to Liz and Ron. What took them to the little town in South Carolina?"

"His work was in Charlotte, but they didn't want to live in the big city. They came upon Park Place by accident when they got lost scouting around for houses one day. They were hungry and bought some sandwich fixings from a grocery store and looked for a place to have a picnic. Park Place Presbyterian has a beautiful courtyard and they stopped in at the church office to ask if they could sit on one of the benches and eat their sandwiches. The church secretary took an immediate liking to them and said it would be fine, but asked them what brought them to Park Place. When they told her they were out looking at houses, she told them that the new parsonage had been built and the church had just put the old one on the market. They looked at it and bought it on the spot. I've always thought it was divine providence. If they had stayed in Charlotte, Liz would have been totally lost when Ron died. Here she had wonderful neighbors to take care of her, which brings me back around to Rock."

"Yeah, I wondered when he was coming into the story."

"Ron and Rock became best friends, playing golf together, fishing together. They were like two peas in a pod. And of course, they included Liz too. They would go out to eat together and he spent a good bit of time with them. They weren't members of his church and I think it felt good to have friends outside his congregation."

"Yeah, I guess if you're a pastor, it's hard to be friends with church members. You'd feel like they were judging your every move."

"Maybe so. But anyway, when Ron died, Rock was a great comfort to Liz and vise-versa. Rock was in his forties but had never been married. There was something about his fiance dying of cancer when they were both seminary students, but I don't know the details. Anyway, the rest is history. Their friendship eventually turned into romance. Liz married Rock two years after Ron passed away, and ten months later they had our little Matthew. The best surprise ever. She and Ron wanted children, but Ron couldn't."

***

Liz had found herself another amazing man, a preacher of a small Presbyterian Church. I found myself wondering why I couldn't have been so lucky. Well, maybe not a preacher, but an amazing man would have been nice. I suppose divorce has a way of changing a woman's perception of love - we're not quite so delusional about having a perfect marriage. Liz's marriage to Ron had been just about as perfect as you get, except they both had wanted babies, but in their case, unlike my own, when they found out they couldn't have any, they loved each other enough. Stan had not loved me enough to be satisfied with a marriage without children. And Liz had now been given a second chance, and Rock seemed like a really nice guy. It had been a sweet marriage ceremony and now that the baby had arrived, I was happy for them.

***

"She's so happy, and of course that makes me happy." Eleanor said. "I wish we lived closer so I could babysit and see them more often."

"It's only a three-hour drive. You can handle that on weekends when you're rid of your sick sister."

"Cassie! You know I don't consider my time with you a burden."

"I know, Eleanor. I was teasing. Looks like you would know by now not to take everything I say literally."

We made record speed until we got to Monroe, then it seemed like a snail's pace until we hit I-485. We arrived at Charlotte Imaging Center a half hour before my appointment, and Simon was waiting for us. Having my own private oncologist is a luxury not many cancer patients have and I teased him about it while we waited for them to call us back. I could tell he's every bit as anxious as I am. We talked about mundane things as they administered the imaging injection, then we waited another hour for it to distribute throughout my body. Next, the scan. The technician's name was Bert and he was young enough to be my son if I had one. It normally takes two to three days for the oncologist to get the results and share them with the patient, but I knew we wouldn't be leaving without knowing. Simon would make sure of that. I'd almost rather not know and I told Simon this.

I think often of the people back before cancer was easily detected and before they had treatment options. It was like that with my grandfather. He complained about feeling bad for about a week and then just dropped dead. Stomach cancer killed him and he just thought he had eaten something that didn't agree with him. That may be the easiest way to go - be sick one day and die the next.

I realized my mind was rambling just as it always does when I get nervous, and I ramble in such morbid ways. But when the scan was finished Simon snapped me out of it.

"Cassie, why don't you go back to the waiting room with Eleanor and Blake while Bert and I review the results? I'll be out shortly."

What do you do when you're waiting for test results? Drum your fingers of course, and Blake, Eleanor and I seemed to be doing it in unison, but we all stopped at the same time when Simon walked back through the door. The look on Simon's face was passive and my stomach dropped just a little bit. I was hoping it would be all smiles and true to my nature, I blurted it out.

"What does that look mean?" I asked, motioning with my finger across my lips in a straight line. "No smile, no frown - what's the verdict."

"Let me give you the good news first," he said.

"So that means there's bad news too?" My optimism level just dropped from the ceiling to the floor.

"Cassie, just be still for a minute so I can tell you. It really is good news."

I stopped pacing to listen. Eleanor held my hand.

"The tumors in the abdominal cavity have shrunk to almost nothing which means the chemo is doing its job."

"So do I have to have more chemo?"

"Yep, I know that's not what you want to hear, and it isn't what I had hoped for. There's still a shadow, and I'm thinking it's just a trace of the tumor that's left. I'm going to change up the chemo a little - treat it a little more aggressively. You can skip this next treatment if you want to. I don't think it will make that much difference to give you another week's rest and let you continue to get your strength back."

"No, I want to get it over with."

"I was hoping you would say that. I do too. We'll get you scheduled for Monday. Meanwhile, I have tomorrow and the rest of the weekend off, unless I'm called to the hospital for an emergency. We'll have time for a rare family get-together."

Eleanor didn't say anything, but I could see big tears forming in her eyes. I found myself comforting her.

"Eleanor, it's not the end of the world. At least the cancer is shrinking and not growing." I kept holding onto her hand and she smiled up at me.

"Of course, you're right," she said. "We have no reason to doubt that you're getting better. God's still in the miracle business."

"Well, I wouldn't put it that way," I said. "I'm not on his miracle recipient list. I tend to trust Simon these days - much more than any old miracles."

Eleanor looked hurt, but she ignored my comment. "We'll stay at your place tonight, Simon, but tomorrow we'll be heading down to Park Place to spend a few days with Liz and Rock. Maybe all of you could come down tomorrow or Sunday and meet the baby?"

"I would love to, and I'm sure Joan would. We live so close and I've been feeling guilty that I haven't even met my new nephew, but I'm on call tomorrow."

"He's your great nephew," I said. "Face it, Simon, we're getting old!"

I was relieved that the focus was no longer on me. I didn't want to cry in front of them and all the other people in the lobby.

It was an unrealistic expectation for me to have hoped that my cancer would have suddenly disappeared, but I had really got my hopes up. Despite my gloominess at the news of more chemo, we all enjoyed our time with Simon and Joan. Joan was a Japanese-American, her soldier father having met her mother during the occupation of Japan after World War II. She's two years older than Simon, and I've always thought she was the best thing that ever happened in his life. She has common sense where he has only genius level sense which doesn't help much in keeping a person grounded. Their children are super smart like Simon, one working at John Hopkins and the other for NASA, neither of them married, but satisfied in their careers.

I think another reason I get along so well with Joan is that she is a no-nonsense person and a little bit outspoken. She doesn't sugar-coat things, not a multicultural trait as being part Japanese, but a locational cultural trait as being Yankeenese - a word I made up especially for her. She makes Eleanor uncomfortable sometimes, I can tell. Eleanor is so culturally Southern to the bone. Politeness is her middle name. As Eleanor was trying so hard to get my mind off the chemo thing, Joan just spit it all out during our dinner conversation and in return, the elephant that was sitting in the background was finally chased out of the room.

"So, Cassie," she said. "Simon tells me you have to go through more chemo. How do you feel about that?"

The focus was back on me, but this time it was a relief to get to explore my feelings on how I really felt about it. I paused, and Eleanor tried to change the subject. "I love your drapes in here, Joan," she gushed. "You must tell me where you got them."

I interrupted. "Eleanor, she was asking me a question. Don't be rude and talk about drapes. I'm sure that like most rich people, she had them custom made, right Joan?"

Joan smiled and nodded. Eleanor blushed and Blake gave me the evil eye for embarrassing his wife.

"I'm sorry, Eleanor," I said. "I know you mean well, but we can't pretend that if we don't talk about my cancer, it will go away. And frankly, Joan, I don't like the results one bit. I'm ready to be done with being sick, but I'm not ready to give up fighting to be well. I'll keep on with the chemo. I trust Simon and I'll do exactly what he says. If I die despite it, I'll come back and haunt him."

Eleanor smiled which made Blake smile which made me smile. They've been so good to me and I don't know what I would do without them.

"As long as Eleanor is willing to make me eat," I said, turning to my sister. "And I'll even go back to your house if you're tired of our little cottage."

"Ha!" she said. "And then I wouldn't be able to see how your love interest plays out. We'll stay right where we are, thank you, ma'am."

Everyone turned to look at me and it was my turn to blush.

"Love interest?" All three of them said it in unison.

"Eleanor has an active imagination", I said. It was my turn to change the subject. "Those drapes really are nice, Joan. Who does your custom work?"

It was one of those knee slapping, bwa-ha-ha kind of laughs that went round the table. The mood had considerably lightened. I love my family! If only Penny could have been there. But she's the only one of us siblings who produced a hearty, plentiful brood of kids. She's busy enough with her five girls, her husband and her fifteen grandkids. Lord, I'm glad I'm not her! Maybe he did reserve a miracle for me after all.

Joan had been such a great hostess, we felt bad just spending one night. She was somehow under the impression we were all staying until Saturday, and was eager to show us Charlotte. What could we do? She had even made reservations at a restaurant uptown with a fabulous view of the Charlotte skyline. I could tell

Eleanor and Blake were chomping at the bits to get on the road, so we made plans to leave early on Saturday morning.

The drive to Park Place was beautiful once we got out of Charlotte. The countryside had changed quite a bit, even since I had been this way for Liz's wedding just a year ago. Huge developments had sprung up where there used to be green pastures. The highway was dotted with big corporations and small businesses alike. Progress, they called it, but I call it a shame. The same was happening in the Raleigh area. The house Stan and I bought when we moved there was once considered out in the country until new developments sprung up all around us. I'm just thankful we bought so much acreage along with it. I thought it silly at the time to buy forty acres, but I guess Stan was forward thinking after all. He was always pretty good at predicting what would turn out to be good financial investments. My property has a huge wrought iron fence all around it, and trees enough to protect my privacy. Too bad he wasn't good at predicting the fate of our marriage, or that he wouldn't get to keep the house he so lovingly built. It would have saved us both a good bit of grief.

When we passed by the Sun's Up Retirement Village, I knew we were getting closer to Park Place and when we pulled into town, I was once again reminded how pretty it is, with the small village atmosphere and the eclectic mix of plantation houses, 1920's bungalows and Victorian mansions. And the pretty old churches scattered throughout the town with bell towers and chimes ringing on the hour. I think I might like to live somewhere like this with its quaint but lively Main Street. It makes you feel like you've stepped back in time to a more genteel way of living. It would be a great place to live, but what Eleanor had said the week before had been spinning around in my mind. The time we had been spending in the little white house this summer had renewed my spirit. There's something about living on the water that is in my family's blood. Penny and Eleanor both have houses in Mt Pleasant; Eleanor's is along the banks of Shem Creek. Eleanor was always begging me to move back to the Lowcountry, and I was beginning to like the idea of living in the house I grew up in.

We finally turned onto Church Street and the church and house came into view. Such a beautiful old brick church! And the house is a large brick house - beautiful, but I think I prefer the one Liz lived in before – the little cottage that sits on the back of the church property. We pulled into the driveway, and I was ever so glad to get out of the car. Blake's backseat had no legroom at all and my legs were cramped.

"We're here!" Eleanor's excitement was contagious. She was so eager to see her only grandson again. She stayed with Liz for a week after he was born, but left to go back home when she sensed Liz and Rock needed their time alone to care for their baby. Even though she denied it, I knew I was the reason she hadn't had a chance to come back.

Eleanor jumped out of the car and headed for the front porch. Blake and I stood beside the car stretching our legs and watching her. The door opened and Liz stepped outside with the baby. Eleanor wrapped both of them in her arms in a flash, and then Rock appeared at the door. I had forgotten how gorgeous he is. Liz lucked up. Of course, as I found out with Stan, looks are deceiving, but this guy was genuine. Eleanor told me about how he handled the difficulties that Liz had in childbirth. A pastor's heart, she calls it. From my experience, not all pastors have it, but then again, Stan always wanted to attend those little obscured denomination churches where all the pastors wanted was your money. He liked having the preachers butter up to him because he gave such a huge amount to the church. The last church we attended together, the pastor disappeared one day along with the church treasurer and the bank account was empty. I suppose the two of them lived happily ever after once they obtained their divorce papers and got married. With those kinds of places as examples, there was little wonder I had become somewhat skeptical when it came to organized religion. We would be visiting Rock's church the next day, and I was curious to see him in action. Eleanor said that God was truly in this place. I had once felt like that, but my recent experiences had been that every time I would walk in the front door of a church, God seemed to run out the back door.

***

"Rock, let's get out of the way here," Blake said. "How about helping me with the luggage while the ladies ooh and ahh over my grandson. It doesn't look like I'm going to get to hold him anytime soon anyway. Nana seems to have dibs on him at the moment."

Eleanor looked up. "But he's sleeping so peacefully in my arms, Blake. You wouldn't want to disturb him, would you?"

"Of course not. I'm just teasing. You've counted the days until you could hold him. I've got plenty of time over the next few days." He turned back to Rock. "I hope it's okay for us to stay through Tuesday? Cassie's chemo is on Monday and then she's due for a shot on Tuesday. Our plan is to take her back to Simon's tomorrow afternoon so she'll be close to the clinic for her appointment on Monday, then Eleanor and I will come back here after we drop her off. It's a longer stay than we planned. I hope it's not an inconvenience?"

"Of course not," Rock said. "It'll make Liz happy. She would like to move you here permanently." He turned to look at me. "I wish you could all stay, but I understand about your need to get back to Charlotte, Cassie. I'm sorry you're having to go through this again. I know you were hoping for better news."

"It's okay," I said. "I knew there was a chance I'd have to have another treatment, but to be honest, I really was hoping they were over. It was a disappointment, but at least I'll get to have the next one in Wilmington. Simon has already arranged it with a cancer clinic there."

"Good! From my experience with cancer patients, riding for long distances is pretty tough after a treatment. The car motion doesn't do your stomach any favors. We're lucky to have a clinic here in town. Our cancer patients in the community used to have to go to Charlotte or Columbia."

"Wow, that's nice. It's such a small town to have a cancer clinic."

"It is. We've got a small hospital too. Dr. Beverly, who donated the facilities for the Beverly Hills Children's Home here in town, also set up a trust fund to include the hospital, and the cancer clinic funding was the brainchild of his grandson who still lives in the area. They're a very generous family and Dr. Beverly's legend lives on in the lives he's touched with his generosity."

"Rock, I have an idea." Liz came up behind him and put her arms around him. It was a sweet, natural gesture and it was easy to see she loved him.

"I love your ideas," he said. "What do you have in mind?"

"Why don't we take Aunt Cassie back to Charlotte tomorrow afternoon and leave Mom and Dad here to babysit? I've been wanting to see Uncle Simon anyway, and while we have babysitters to take advantage of, we could eat in a nice restaurant while we're there."

"I have a better idea," Blake said. "Why don't you two spend the night in Charlotte? You had such a short honeymoon last year, and your vacation at the beach this year was cut short, I'm sure some time together, just the two of you would be nice."

"Oh, Blake - you have the best ideas." Eleanor was practically jumping for joy. "Please, Liz, let us keep him overnight!"

"Are you sure, Mom? You haven't been around babies in years."

"She's babysat Penny's kids all these years, and even Penny's grandkids. Besides, she has that mothering instinct, Liz," Blake said. "And between the two of us, what could possibly go wrong?"

Rock laughed. "Famous last words," he said. "Liz, honey, I'm alright with it if you are."

"Hmm...," she said. "For now, we'll plan on the eating out thing. I'll have to think about leaving my little munchkin overnight."

If I had been a betting woman, I would have wagered right then and there that spending the night away from the baby wasn't going to happen.

"Okay," Rock said. "One thing at a time. Let's get those bags in, Blake. Then I'll show you to your bedrooms. We'll eat a light lunch because Liz has a huge pot roast ready to put in the oven for dinner."

"I hope she uses her mother's recipe for pot roast. It's the best I've ever had."

"Must be," Rock said. "It's my favorite." He patted his stomach. "You can see that my lean bachelor days are over. I've changed belt sizes twice since we've been married."

Liz laughed. "Y'all just don't know the half of it. Half the women in our church were feeding him, most of them mothers of single daughters trying to snare the most eligible bachelor in Park Place."

"Yep," I said. "Probably a few divorcees too. If I lived here and could cook worth a hoot, I probably would have been one of them." Rock blushed and Liz laughed.

"Don't pay attention to her, Rock." Eleanor said, laughing. "Cassie plays her cancer card well - she thinks it gives her a license to say anything she wants to say and get away with it."

"They know I'm kidding, Eleanor. Besides, I'm a good ten years older than my sweet niece's husband."

"Actually, he's closer to your age than mine," Liz said. "You're only three or four years older than him."

"My Gosh, Liz," I said. "You married an old man!"

"Tell me about it," Rock said. "I'll be in my mid-sixties when our Matthew graduates from high school."

I love my family. We have such a sweet way of insulting each other.

CHAPTER 14

I didn't have any dressy clothes to bring from the beach so I had nothing really suitable to wear to church. I thought it was a good excuse to just skip out while the others went, but Liz wouldn't hear of it.

"You're about the size I was before I got pregnant," she said. "I can't wear any of my pre-pregnancy clothes yet, so you've got lots to choose from."

She was right, and she had some killer clothes. I found something right away that fit and it looked so good on me that I decided I did want to go to church after all to show off my new look. My dress clothes at home were two or three sizes too big now. If it hadn't been the cancer that had caused my weight loss, I would be totally happy with my new thin figure. With shoes and purse to match, I was feeling quite chic when I walked into the church with Eleanor and Blake. Liz and little Matthew walked in ahead of us and we all sat on the front row which I had never done in my whole life. Matthew soon fell sound asleep with Eleanor holding him. I'm sure she didn't hear a word of the sermon because she stared down at him the whole time with a silly grin on her face.

Rock's sermon made me squirm a little bit, especially when he read the scripture from John about Nicodemus. I guess I'm a little like Nicodemus because I've never understood the part about no one can see the Kingdom of God unless he's born again. Unlike old Nic, I do know what born again means, but I've always thought it was one of those "aha" moments and I've never had one of those. We grew up going to church every Sunday, and as a child I never doubted that God was real. I had a little trouble understanding the trinity back then, but after a while, I got it. But after years of not going to church and turning my back on God because I thought he turned his back on me, I had a somewhat defeatist attitude and thought, if I have to be born again to get to heaven, I'm afraid it's a little too late. I didn't like the part he read about darkness though. Maybe I would read John over again someday.

Rock asked us to stand with him as he greeted the church members as they filed out the door. It's easy to see why he's so loved by his congregation. He knows each one of them by name, who their children are, and the struggles they've been going through. He doesn't just stand there and shake hands, he really cares. A lady named Maura apparently knew they were having guests. She and a few other ladies had prepared lunch and brought it over to us shortly after we got back to the house. I was beginning to think I should be a preacher's wife if people cook for you all the time.

After lunch, Liz took Blake and Eleanor back to the nursery and gave them a mini-course in babysitting, as if they needed it. Penny's adult kids learned early on that Eleanor loved babies and when the real grandma couldn't keep her grandchildren, their Aunt Eleanor would. It's a good thing they didn't have to rely on their Aunt Cassie. They would never get a break.

The others left me and Rock to do the dishes. I didn't mind. I wanted to ask him a few questions about his sermon, especially the part about being born again.

"Cassie, some people have those aha moments as you call them, and some people seem to just grow into it. They're born of the Spirit and don't remember having any kind of aha moment. For those open to God's message, Jesus sends his Spirit, The Holy Spirit, thus being born from above, born of the Spirit as the scripture passage reads.

People who have evil in their hearts love darkness, they think it hides their evil from others. But people who live by the truth, they come into the light, in this case the light is Jesus."

"I hate darkness," I said. "Does that mean I don't have evil in my heart? What if I don't have the Spirit in my heart? Will I have to live in darkness when I die?"

"You've asked some good questions, Cassie. Whether you know it now or not, it means you're searching for answers. Come on into my study and we'll talk more."

Uh, oh. What am getting myself into, I thought as I followed him into his office, which was probably meant to be a den or library. There was a large bookcase on one wall and it held a huge collection of books, most of them in the genre of religion. He picked up two small paperbacks and talked to me in depth about his sermon.

"Since I don't live near enough to counsel with you, I've got some good reading material for you. But truthfully, it's not something you have to pour over, day and night. You don't have to dig deep into theology. You just have to pray a prayer of forgiveness and accept Jesus into your heart." He thumbed through one of the books. "This is a commentary on the Book of John. John's gospel is a good place to start." He handed both books to me. He was looking at me expectantly. "Would you be open to sitting with me now and talking through it? Like I said, just a simple prayer can bring you into the light."

"Thanks, Rock. I'll read them. I'm not ready. I still have to come to grips with my attitude towards God."

He squeezed my hand gently and smiled. "Just don't wait too long."

***

Rock and Liz drove me back to Charlotte late in the afternoon. I was exhausted, and when we got to Simon's, I used the excuse of needing a nap while they all visited with each other. All I really needed was to have a pity party and I needed to be alone to have it. Maybe I should have taken a break between treatments and waited for a couple of weeks. Why had the cancer not just disappeared? That's what everyone said they were praying for. I had even sneaked in a prayer or two myself, just in case. Now I was going to have to go through the nausea and feeling wrung out all over again. I got out my cell phone thinking if I talked it out with someone, I would feel better, but I just thumbed through all my contacts and stared at the phone. Who could I call? I realized that my friendships in Raleigh didn't really have any substance to them. They were country club friends, book club friends, garden club friends and gals to shop with. How many clubs could one person belong to? They would be totally bored and would maybe feign interest for a while if I shared my blue moments with them, but they really didn't care. Rock and Liz were lucky to have people in their church to care for them. I started feeling envious. Maybe I should join a church for no other reason than to have someone care. I scrolled through my contacts one more time. The only person I had any desire to talk to was Carl, and I didn't even have his number. I brushed my teeth and put my pajamas on. It was too early to go to bed, but I tucked myself in anyway with the intention of reading one of Rock's books. I woke up at six a.m. with the book still in my hand. I must have been more exhausted than I thought. It was time to get up and get ready for my poisoning appointment. I wondered what kind of toxins would flow through my blood this time.

CHAPTER 15

Eleanor and I settled into our normal routines when we got back to our home away from home. The chemo hadn't been any worse than the other times, and the injection that followed the next day was old hat by now. The technician did say that when the chemo built up in my bloodstream, I may be sick again like I was during the first few months. I hoped not. My bones were aching again from the shot and all I wanted to do was stay in bed. Eleanor would have none of that, so we got in a routine of driving down to the beach, taking our chairs, an umbrella and a cooler along with us. My nausea was kept in check, and I was craving peanut butter and jelly sandwiches, but not much else. She would pack our lunch and we would stay almost all day, having easy access to the public restrooms where we parked.

Each day I took my notebook along with me, and the words were flowing. Before I knew it, I had the makings of a sweet little book about a misguided love story. I would come home each evening and type up what I had handwritten during the day. When I had five chapters done, I had Eleanor edit it and I emailed it to my agent right away. I was afraid she would be upset because it was nothing like the books I had been writing, but two days later, I got a phone call from her telling me she loved it and was pitching it to a different publisher.

"What's come over you, Cassie? This is good stuff. I thought you were dying."

"I might yet," I said.

"Well, it's making you write better, so go for it!"

"Do you think it will sell?"

"Maybe. If we can advertise it as your last book - written on your deathbed."

This is why I love my agent. She's just as sarcastic as I am. "But what if I don't die", I said. My reputation will be ruined. They'll accuse me of falsifying my prognosis to promote my book."

"Don't worry, I'll think of something. I'm trying to figure out what genre to put it under. Tell me how you're thinking it will end."

"I don't know yet. I'm still living it out."

"You mean it's a true story and this guy is for real? Blue eyes and all? Maybe I should come down there."

"No, you would ruin my chances. You're ten years younger than me and you're not sick."

"How is he handling your cancer? The "Big C" as you like to call it?"

"He doesn't know."

"What! It's going to have a lousy ending, I just know it. You'd better come up with a happy ending. People don't like broken hearts."

"Sometimes they do. Look at Dr. Zhivago - that was the saddest ending I've ever read and it sold millions. And Albus Dumbledore in Harry Potter. It broke everyone's heart when he died."

"I thought you'd never read Harry Potter."

"I haven't, but I read reviews, you know. I wanted to find out why those books sold so well. I still don't know. They sound dreadful."

"If only I could have been *her* agent!" She sounded so morose, I kind'a felt sorry for her. But then she had to add on to the sentence, "instead of yours." I hung up on her, but she called me back.

"You know I'm kidding," she said. "Just keep writing. And make it have a happy ending!" It was her turn to hang up.

***

On Friday, we decided to just hang out at the house. It was hot and Eleanor was sunburned. I had seen very little of Carl. We had been gone most of the week and I couldn't keep up with his comings and goings. His truck was gone for a couple of days after we got home from Charlotte, and when it reappeared, he was in and out with his boat. When I did see him, he would just wave and go in the house, not coming out again until the next morning when he would go out in his boat. I had a feeling he was trying to cool things down with our relationship and I was beginning to wonder if I had just imagined the kisses and the sparks flying. Meanwhile the news channels were reporting that two shrimp boat captains off the Florida coast had been arrested for bringing in bales of marijuana and the search was on for their source. Could this have anything to do with Carl? Maybe that's why he was ignoring me and was gone so much.

"Stop dreaming up stuff, Cassie," I said out loud. I was on the gazebo reading the newspaper account of the arrests. I had been so engrossed in my reading, that I hadn't heard the footsteps on the dock below.

"Dreaming of me, I hope."

I was startled and looked down to see a pair of sexy blue eyes looking up at me. His smile was teasing. No wonder I hadn't heard him - he didn't have his shoes on.

"Well there's the barefooted stranger," I said. "I was beginning to wonder if you were still our neighbor." He started walking up the stairs to the gazebo.

"Same here. You and your sister leave early and come back late every day, or at least on the days I've been here."

I laughed. "We've discovered the beach. It's addicting." He was standing in front of me and I felt a tingling sensation from head to toe. He was looking straight into my eyes and I thought I might melt.

"I thought so too, the last time I was on the beach... with you. I've missed you."

I blushed and couldn't think of a single word to say.

"I was getting ready to take the boat out to Bird Island. Would you like to ride with me?"

Of course, I wanted to scream. But I got up slowly and started for the door. I had already, that quickly, dismissed my earlier suspicions of him and I made up my mind he was innocent. Or maybe my attraction to him was blinding me to his faults. Whatever! I wasn't going to miss going on a boat ride with him. "Sure, I'll just go in and let Eleanor know where we're going."

"I'll be waiting."

When I got down to the dock, he was putting his shoes on. "Wait, let me help you in the boat." I waited, which was out of character for me. I would have normally said that I'm perfectly capable of getting into a boat and jumped in. There's no wonder I've been a big turn-off for men. I don't allow them to be chivalrous. Since Stan, I've just never met one that made me care.

His boat was a perfect size for the ocean or waterway - a 21 footer. The color was almost a camouflaged color. Not your typical forest camo, but a deep sea blue and green pattern. I figured it must be a custom color - almost as if he doesn't want to be seen. Equipped with a center console and a bench seat, the 250hp Mercury outboard engine was a lot of power for the size of the boat. I looked over at my rental boat that I had been neglecting lately. The beach had been taking up too much of our time. It was a 16 footer with a 50hp engine, as much as anyone needs in the waterway or on a calm ocean.

He took the waterway route and drove slowly. We talked about the large houses being built on the mainland side. The island side had developed rapidly since the 1990's, but the opposite side had only recently drawn interest with builders. We talked in an easy banter, both agreeing that if we had the choice, we would prefer living on the waterway than on the oceanfront. The dunes were too fragile to protect the houses from major storms on the ocean side.

We weren't in any hurry, just enjoying the scenery and each other's company. Or at least I hoped he was enjoying being with me. Boats passed us on the right and left, seemingly in a hurry to get somewhere. I wanted to take all the time in the world. I had looked back behind us a couple of times and noticed one boat seemed to be going at our same pace. It was a large boat and could have easily overtaken us.

"I think we're being followed", I said, jokingly. Carl looked back and slowed down. The boat slowed too. He sped up and the other boat sped up, keeping the same distance behind us. He didn't say anything, but I noticed that he seemed to tense up.

"Have you had dinner?" he asked.

"I had a banana about an hour ago," I said. "Eleanor had just made a salad when I left. I told her to put mine in the fridge until we got back from our boat ride."

"I haven't either and I didn't realize how hungry I was until I got out on the boat. We're not far from the Inlet View. Let's stop and eat there. I'm craving some crab cakes. We'll still have time to go on to Bird Island where we can watch the sun set. It's just below Sunset Beach, right where the shoreline does its final curve to the West before it starts going South again toward Myrtle Beach. The sunsets are spectacular." He looked behind us again, then turned to me. "Is that okay with you?"

"Sure, I can eat anytime. I'm hungry too."

He rumbled his hand around in the dash. "I have some snacks in here, but I don't think that will hold us. If we don't eat now, we'll be starved by the time we get back from Bird Island."

When we pulled into the dock at the restaurant, I looked behind us. The other boat had disappeared. He noticed it too and seemed relieved.

The last time we were at the restaurant, we were with Eleanor and Blake. I was looking at it with new eyes, having Carl all to myself. The name of the restaurant tells most of the story. It's at a small inlet on the Shallotte River near the mouth of the ocean. This time around, the view was even more incredible and the food was even better. I had a flounder sandwich and he had crab cakes and a small salad, both washed down with at least a half-gallon of sweet tea. I took a bathroom break before we left while he went back down to the boat. He was standing beside the boat when I came down.

"Cassie, did you notice this scratch before we left?" he asked, pointing out a diagonal scratch about a foot long on the starboard side of the boat.

"Gosh, that's so apparent, I'm sure I would have noticed it," I said. I'm 99% sure it wasn't there when we got in the boat at the dock. It looks like someone has purposely keyed it. I don't think another boat could have done that kind of scratch."

"That's what I thought," he said. He looked concerned but then seemed to shake it off. "Well, let's get going if we're going to have time to explore the island." He helped me in and I let him.

We picked up the pace a little as we cruised past Ocean Isle. Bird Island was once separated from Sunset Beach by a narrow inlet, but over time it has filled in and people can easily walk from Sunset to the pristine beaches of the little island that's owned by the state of North Carolina.

We pulled the boat on shore on the waterway side and got out, tying it to a large log that had washed up on the island. The island is narrow so we were able to quickly walk to the ocean side.

"This used to be a nude beach," he said with a grin.

"Well, don't get any ideas," I said.

He laughed. "I would probably run in the other direction if I saw someone nude approaching us," he said.

"Well, be sure to take me with you. Don't leave me with the loonies."

He took my hand. "I'd better hold on to you, just in case."

We walked hand in hand for about fifteen minutes, not seeing another person in sight. He had brought a towel from the boat and spread it down on the sand. "It's not very big," I said as he was spreading it out.

"It'll force you to sit close to me," he said. He sat down and pulled me down beside him. I leaned into him as he put his left arm around me. I could feel his heartbeat and it was racing just as fast as mine. This probably wasn't a good idea. As if the gulls could read my thoughts, they came flying in all around us, making both of us laugh. "They think we have something to eat," he said.

"We should have brought some hushpuppies from the restaurant." I tried shooing them away. "As long as they don't poop in my hair, I'll be glad to share space with them," I said.

"Uh oh, one just did," he said. He laughed as I screamed and started running my fingers through my hair. "That's not very smart. You'll get it all over your hands." I stopped, horrified. "Just kidding," he said.

"You're incorrigible," I said, swatting my hand at him. He grabbed it.

"And you're beautiful when you're mad," he said. He turned loose of my hand and pulled my hair back from my face. He pulled me to him and our lips met. The kiss was lingering, exploring, and I could have gotten lost in it, but he pulled back. "And I can't be doing that, again," he said. "I don't want to stop." I knew what he meant. I didn't either.

There were lots of shells on the beach, a small batch of them had been deposited by the waves and were within easy reach of the towel. I sifted through them with my left hand, and came across a piece of sea glass, polished smooth over the years with the constant tumbling in the sea by Mother Nature. I lifted it up trying to see through it, but the cobalt blue was too frosty. I put it up to Carl's cheek.

"Feel how smooth it is?" I said, rubbing it across the stubble on his face. I let go, but he grabbed my hand back and kissed one finger at a time, then the back of my hand. I sighed, then shook myself. My feelings were getting way out of control, so I pulled my hand away, dropping the seaglass on the sand.

He picked it up. "Beautiful," he said, "like you." He started to hand it back to me.

I had pulled myself back together, and laughed. "Keep it," I said. "It'll remind you that I look like a rock."

He put it in his pocket. "It'll remind me of this night... with you." His magnetic eyes pulled mine back to his. "You won't let anyone give you a compliment, will you?"

I shrugged. It's true. I always have a comeback when someone tries to compliment me. My psychiatrist would say it's a self-esteem problem from being rejected. I say, I'm just a realist, forget the psyche! It was becoming uncomfortable to sit straight up without anything supporting my back so I leaned back against his chest. He rubbed my neck in soft little strokes.

"When will you be going back to Raleigh?" he asked.

"In about three weeks, I think. I'll have to ask Eleanor how long she's rented the house for. I think through the end of August."

"Cassie, I want to keep seeing you after you go back. That is, if you want to."

"I do," I said, and I really meant it. "You know, I don't even have your phone number. I wanted to call you when I was in Charlotte. I have a hundred people in my address book but the only person I wanted to talk to was you."

He looked pleased. "We can fix that," he said. "Where's your phone?" I took it out of my pocket and handed it to him and watched as he put his number as a contact.

"What did you want to talk about? Anything important, or just talk?"

I paused. He turned my face around and looked me in the eye. "Won't you tell me?" He looked concerned.

I sighed. "I was feeling down and I realized I don't have any real friends. I have shopping buddies, book club and other organizational type friends, but no one to really share being blue with. I have family, but they don't need my problems."

"Do you have church friends you can lean on when you're down?"

"No." I didn't elaborate.

He pulled me closer. "I want you to share things with me. The good and the bad. Are you okay now? Do you still need to talk things out?"

"I don't know... Yes, I need to tell you something."

"Anything," he said.

I looked at him and tried to gauge what his reaction would be. But then I just blurted it out. It wasn't fair to keep it from him any longer.

"I have cancer." There, I'd said it. I had a fleeting thought that he would get up and walk away, but he didn't. He sat there and stared at me with those eyes. Eyes that looked as if they could see into my soul. And what he said next made me wonder if maybe they could.

"I know."

I pulled away and turned to face him in disbelief. "You know! And you're not running away? How?"

He pulled me back. "Blake told me - the second time he came down. I think he was just trying to protect you."

"So you felt sorry for me which is why you've been kind to me!" I started to get up, but he pulled me back down.

"Cassie, are you kidding me! Is that what you think? I like to think that I'm kind to everyone, and I don't go around kissing people I feel sorry for. There's nothing about you or your personality that I feel sorry for. It's not your cancer that defines you. You're strong willed, independent, beautiful, witty...." He paused for a second, "and kissable." He kissed me again, a peck on the cheek. "Did you know that one in four people will get cancer in their lifetime? I could get cancer tomorrow. I hate that you have it, Cassie, but seeing how you've handled it has made me admire you more, and as you can see, it doesn't turn me off." He lifted the hair off the back of my shoulders and kissed my neck. His breath was so warm I couldn't help but shiver. "I want you to get well. I want to keep seeing you."

"But I'm not handling it very well right now," I said. "And I was having a full scale pity party the night I wanted to call you. I was hoping for no more chemo, but...."

"I know. I called Blake."

"You what!"

"He gave me his number so I could call him if there was an emergency with you or Eleanor."

"But...."

"And I figured when you said you were going to Charlotte, you must be going for tests, so I called him on Monday when you didn't come home. He told me the results of the PET scan. I'm sorry, Cassie. And being sorry that you're going through this is different than feeling sorry for you."

I tried to hold up, but I broke down and the tears spilled forth. I cried softly and his arms tightened around me and he held me close until my crying jag was over. I know I must have looked a mess. Crying turns my face all red and splotchy, but he didn't seem to notice. It was the first time I had really cried in front of anybody in over fifteen years - well, since Stan left and I made a fool of myself in front of him, my family and all my friends. But this time, I didn't feel foolish. I felt cleansed and good.

"Simon, my brother...did Blake tell you about Simon?" He nodded. "Well anyway, Simon doesn't seem too concerned. He thinks the new strength of chemo will get rid of the remaining cells totally. But if not, he'll do radiation." I tried to put on my bravest face. Simon had told me that some of my up and down emotional issues were part of the hormonal changes from having my ovaries removed.

"I do feel better about it, really." And I did, but knowing that he knew and had known all along was throwing me for a loop. And here, I'd been trying to find a way to tell him.

"So do I, Cassie. I've been praying for you ever since Blake told me."

"What?"

Carl laughed. "If you keep opening your mouth so wide and saying 'what', something's going to fly in."

"I'm just in shock. I didn't know you prayed."

"Why? Oh, because you don't trust me, right?"

"Well, you haven't exactly been upfront with me, have you? You're here one day and then you disappear for several. And you won't tell me what you do for a living. I know you have to have a job."

He hung his head. "And I still can't tell you what I do for a living. That's why I don't let myself get close to anybody. There's always too many questions. Is it too much to ask for you to trust me? For now, anyway."

What was he hiding? It was just too frustrating. "Do criminals pray?" I asked. "How can I trust you when I'm wondering if you're involved in something illegal? I don't want to think that, but..."

"Hey," he said, standing up and pulling me up with him. "Let's don't let this ruin what we came out here for.

He looked at his watch and then to the sky. "We have just enough time to walk down to the rock jetty and watch the sunset. I've been told that this is the prettiest place on the East Coast to see it."

"Well, I'm game," I said, walking ahead of him. "I wouldn't want to ruin your chance of seeing a fabulous sunset. Who knows, the next time you see one, it may be through the bars of a jail cell."

He laughed. "Now that's the Cassie I've come to know. I'll race you."

"You'll win," I said.

"Better yet, hop on my shoulders and I'll carry you."

"I've never turned down a free ride," I said. He stooped down low enough for me to straddle his shoulders. He started running.

"Whee," I said. "Run Forrest, run!" It was silly, but it suited the lighter moment. As he ran through the sand with me on his back, I felt light as a feather. There was no way he could have carried me on his shoulders before I got sick. It made me want to stay thin. Not sickly thin, but healthy thin. It would give me an incentive to eat healthier. I kind of liked riding on his shoulders.

When we reached the jetty, he bent his knees to the ground so I could get down. The western sky was already beginning to turn exceptional colors. The whispy clouds were tinged with shades of pink and orange mingling amongst the soft blue of the sky. The ocean was a mirrored reflection of all the beauty of the soon to be setting sun. The evening star was visible just to the upper left of the sun.

We stood there in silence, occasionally letting out an ooh or an ahh. Then he put his arm around my shoulder. "It reminds me of a poem by Tennyson," he said. "I think I remember the first verse or two."

"Sunset and evening star
    And one clear call for me!
And may there be no moaning of the bar,
    When I put out to sea,

"But such a tide as moving seems asleep,
    Too full for sound and foam,
When that which drew from out the boundless deep
    Turns again home."

"That's all I remember," he said, with an embarrassed laugh.

"I know the rest," I said. "I've always identified with that poem. The sea is in my blood, growing up on the edge of it as we did. This is the how I quoted it in our English class in tenth grade." I stood up straight and put my hand over my heart.

"Twilight and evening bell,
    And after that the dark!
And may there be no sadness of farewell,
    When I embark;

For though from out our bourne of Time and Place
    The flood may bear me far,
I hope to see my Pilot face to face

When I have crossed the bar."

"Very dramatic," he said, and I laughed.

"I've always thought that when my time comes, I want to go like that. Just put my body in a little Jon boat and push me out to sea."

"I don't think they let you do things like that," he said.

"I'm pretty sure they don't, but they should." His hand went from my shoulder to my waist and I leaned into him.

He was right. The sunset was incredible, made even more incredible by being in the arms of a man I had fallen hopelessly in love with. And hopeless, it was. I knew he cared about me as a friend, well, maybe a little more than a friend, but he could never feel about me the way I felt about him. Cassie, oh Cassie! Whatever have you done?

The ride home was quiet. He seemed to appreciate the stillness of gliding through the backwaters at night as much as I did. The darkness makes you more aware of the sounds around you. Deer love the coastal area because the vegetation and scrubby pines are so thick. They have no trouble hiding during the day and wait for nightfall to feed. But boating in the dark is not for the fainthearted and I always shudder when I hear things slithering in the marsh grass, the alligator's natural habitat. As we entered the channel at Shallotte River, Carl turned off the engine and was using only the trolling motor. The boat traffic was almost nil, and suddenly I heard a sound like someone swimming and splashing alongside us.

"A dolphin," Carl said. "Two dolphins!" There was one on each side of the boat as if they were guiding us in. They stayed that way until we crossed over the Lockwood Folly Inlet, then they ventured on out to sea. It had been a long time since I had experienced such complete unabandoned happiness. The coastal backwaters are where I belong. I decided to put my house in Raleigh on the market as soon as I got home. Our old home place was calling my name.

CHAPTER 16

Carl and his boat were gone when I got up on Saturday morning. And still gone when Eleanor and I left for Wilmington for my chemo treatment on Monday morning. So much for trusting him. He could have at least told me he was leaving.

It was an easy ride to Wilmington. The clinic was near the hospital and Eleanor knew exactly how to get there. She had driven up from Charleston earlier in the summer when Liz's pregnancy had been threatened while she and Rock were on vacation. The clinic was nice and seemed to be run by very competent technicians. Just as in Charlotte and Raleigh, I was to return the next morning to check my blood cell count and to get an injection if I needed it. Eleanor suggested that we stay overnight so we wouldn't have to make the hour trip back and then the same trip the next morning. I agreed, but we didn't have an overnight bag with us. A good excuse to do some shopping, Eleanor said. Any excuse to shop is fine with me and I wouldn't feel like doing anything in the middle of the week. If the nausea came back, it would be the second or third day after my treatment. I was in bad need of some new clothes. The few things I had brought from home were almost worn out from washing and drying so much. We found a hotel in Wrightsville Beach and hit the malls.

It's funny what a new outfit will do for your self-esteem. Back at the hotel, we gussied ourselves up, then dined early at the Bluewater Waterfront Grill. We got a nice table with a water view and had good food, good service and fun people-watching.

***

Since we were able to get in and out of the clinic quickly the next morning, we ate lunch on the way home and got back to the cottage a little after 1 pm. Carl's boat was back at the dock. I was getting fed up with wondering where this man was all the time and to be truthful, I was mad at myself for walking on eggshells with him and even madder that I cared so much. I saw that the Lady Lu was back and docked in front of the fish house.

"I'll come back after my things," I told Eleanor. "I want to go see Captain Chuck."

"Go ahead, I'll have to make more than one trip anyway, so I'll bring yours in too."

"Thanks." I ran down the steps, but slowed down when I got about mid-way down. The nausea was hitting me quicker this time than it had during my other treatments. Simon said it would be a stronger dose. My stomach settled as I walked at a slower pace. Chuck watched me from the back of the boat where he was putting ice in the hold. He came out to greet me.

"You're a little grey faced this afternoon. Are you feeling okay?"

I nodded. "Just had chemo yesterday - a newer and stronger poison."

"I was hoping you were finished with that."

"Me too," I said. I didn't need to explain. He'd been down that road before."

"I wondered where you were. We got in yesterday and I didn't see any lights on in your house. I'm glad you got back before I left. As soon as Red and Johnny get here, we're headin' on out. We probably won't be back until Friday."

He no sooner got the words out of his mouth, when Red's girlfriend drove up. Red got out of the passenger side, and Johnny from the back seat.

"Just a little word of warning," Chuck said. "The Black Jack is supposed to come in sometime today. Keep your doors locked."

"Thanks for the warning," I said. I watched as the boys walked around the fish house to the dock. "How's Johnny working out?" I asked.

Chuck smiled. "Excellent," he said. "All he needs is a little hard work and a smidgen of guidance."

"And you're the best one to orchestrate it," I said.

He seemed embarrassed by my comment and looked down at his hands, scraped and calloused by working the net. "I don't know about that. I can work him hard, but the guidance seems to be coming more from the church he's attending now, the one he went to as a child, the one he grew away from as a young man. We should all be so lucky to be welcomed back into the fold."

"I'm glad he's getting the attention he needs. Hey, I gotta go. I'll see you Friday."

"If the good Lord's willing and the creek don't rise," he said.

"Hey, my daddy used to say that. I haven't heard it in a long time."

The boys walked up and I waved goodbye.

As I walked up the stairs from the dock, I saw Carl coming to greet me.

"Wait up," he said, walking faster. I just kept walking as if I didn't hear him.

"Cassie, wait up," he said again. This time I stopped and waited for him, but didn't offer him a smile when his blue eyes locked on mine.

"Well the wandering boy has returned," I said, with my best bite of sarcasm.

"I'm sorry," he said. "I can explain."

"Please do." I just stood there with my arms crossed.

"Something came up and I had to leave quickly," he said. "I..."

"Oh, that's a jolly good excuse," I said. I turned around and stomped toward the house.

"Cassie, listen to me." He was pleading now, but I had no sympathy. I stopped in my tracks and turned around to face him. I'm sure there was steam coming off the top of my head.

"Oh, I've listened to you, alright. I listened to you when you carried me off into the sunset. I listened to you when you said you'd been praying for me. I even stupidly let you kiss me and felt it to the bottom of my toes. But if you don't have the common decency to at least tell me that you're leaving and will be gone for days, I'm through listening to you."

He looked sad and I almost melted, but I didn't. He put his arm out toward me and I slapped it away, turned on my heels and slammed the screen door behind me.

I actually felt better for saying what I felt. I would just ignore him from now on. The more I fumed, the more drama I added to what I was going to do. I was even going to ask Simon to find me a cancer clinic in Charleston and I would go back home with Eleanor instead of being on an emotional roller coaster here so close to Carl. Ha! That would show him.

I walked into the kitchen and there was a note from Eleanor. "I've gone to the store to pick up some bread."

I was thankful for the quiet time. I didn't want her to see me so upset. I rummaged in the fridge and found some ginger ale to settle my stomach, then sat down at the table. I thought about the afternoon on Bird Island and the feelings Carl had stirred up in me. I hadn't felt that way in years - heck, I'd never felt that way. Stan and I had met our senior year in college and me, being the little backwoods country girl, was impressed with his family's money. And he, being a wealthy prince charming was enchanted with my Cinderella story. I had never looked in Stan's eyes and got lost. And I had never had the feelings for him that I already had for Carl.

I heard footsteps on the deck outside the back door. Hoo-boy, I thought. What am I going to say if he comes back and apologizes? I got up from the table and was all set to rush to the door, but I'm glad I looked out first. It floored me to see Jack Crum striding toward the door looking furtively back over his shoulder.

Oh my gosh, I hadn't heard his shrimp boat come in. What could I do? I didn't want him to know I was alone. I stepped away from the center of the kitchen. He couldn't see me if I ducked around the corner to the sink. Had I locked the door? Oh, God, help me - I hadn't! In my hurry to make a statement after my tiff with Carl, I had come inside and slammed the screen door behind me, not thinking to lock it. Carl and Chuck had both told me that Jack was dangerous and to keep it locked.

I looked quickly around for a weapon, maybe a knife or something, but my efficient sister always dried and put everything away, and the utensil drawer in the cottage was strangely over near the refrigerator, an odd place for sure. Where was Eleanor's sterling silver serving fork when I needed it? Or one of her fancy chef knives?

My gosh, he hadn't even knocked and was opening the door. But what else could I expect from the creepy man? Did I think he was coming to a tea party? It was too late to make a dash for the front door, and regretfully I had a sickening feeling what Dirty Jack had in mind. Chuck had warned me: Carl had warned me. Why had I not locked the screen door? It would have at least given me a chance to run for help.

"God, what can I do?" I said frantically. Suddenly, it came to me. I heard footsteps getting closer. He was trying to walk quietly so as to catch me by surprise. I turned back to the sink and jammed my fingers down my throat. It worked. With the stronger chemo, I was one step away from throwing up anyway. My lunch gushed out in the sink and the only thing I could think of was to smear it on my chin and on my hands, making me gag even more. I heard him come into the kitchen, and said under my breath, "Lord, if I can pull this off, I'll go to church on Sunday and sit on the front row."

I could smell the stench of him, which was another gagging factor, and I knew he was almost to me. Then he spoke.

"Well, if it isn't the pretty little slut, all alone. I saw your friend's car pull out of the driveway, then saw you and your boyfriend having a spat. Here's Jack at your service, girlie."

Okay, it was now or never. I turned to face him and the lear on his face turned to disgust when he saw I was covered in vomit.

"What is wrong with you?" he said, pulling back.

It was time to put on a show. I was always the drama queen, and it was time to do or die.

"What do you think is wrong with me?" I screamed. "I'm sure you've heard by now; everyone else has!"

"Wha...what?"

"I've got AIDS, man! I'm dying. That's what!"

His look of disgust turned to horror. I slung the sickening stuff off my hand towards him. It landed on his shoe.

"Uh, oh", I said. "You know that it's spread by bodily fluids, don't you?"

He looked down at his foot and screamed, "You got it on my shoe, you little witch!"

I thought he was going to hit me. He raised back his fist, but then looking at my icky face, thought better of it and took off running out the door, the screen slamming behind him. I watched as he took off his shoe and flung it into the murky water below.

I heard another set of footsteps then, and heard Carl's raised voice. "What are you doing on this porch?"

"Get out of my way!" Jack shouted. "And don't get near that slut if you know what's good for you."

I heard a scuffle on the deck with some obscenities thrown in. I quickly washed my face and hands and rinsed my mouth out. It was making me sick to be sick. I opened the cabinet door over the sink and saw the box of baking soda. I made a paste of it and rubbed it over my teeth and gargled. At least it took away the icky taste. Then out of sheer physical and mental exhaustion, I sat down right where I was on the floor. I wrapped my arms around my knees, then lowered my head and sobbed.

I heard Carl frantically calling my name. "Cassie, where are you?"

"I'm in the kitchen," I said, weakly. He ran to me and knelt down on the floor beside me. He pulled my head up and looked me in the eyes.

"Did he hurt you?"

I shook my head, no. "No, he didn't touch me." I started sobbing again, and he pulled me into his arms and held me close.

"Shh.., it's okay, Cassie. Just cry it out." I cried for longer than I should have because, frankly, I was enjoying being in his arms. I felt protected and that's something my independent self hasn't felt since I was a kid.

He pulled me away from him slightly, long enough to look at me. "I was so afraid when I saw him running out of the house. I just knew he had hurt you and I was ready to... well, I don't know what I would have done." He held me close again. This time I pulled away, taking the paper towel I had dried my hands with and blew my nose.

He looked at me with a confused expression. "What did you do to him to cause him to run out of the house like his pants were on fire? And why did he throw his shoe in the water?" I straightened up. I realized just then that God had come through for me. I had to give Him credit for my quick thinking.

"Cassie?" he asked again. "What made him leave?"

I looked at him with a faint smile. "I made myself throw up and told him I was dying of AIDS. Then I slung throw-up on his shoe."

Again, he looked confused, then incredulous, then started laughing until he snorted. The sheer craziness of the moment made me laugh with him, but then he got serious.

He pulled me up and sat me in a chair, then sat in the chair beside me, holding me by the shoulders, looking at my disheveled appearance. "Are you sure you're alright?"

I nodded. "But now I've got to go to church on Sunday. I promised."

"Promised who? Jack?" he said with astonishment.

"No. God. I made a deal with Him."

He sighed with relief. "Well, you sure can't renege on your promise to God," he said. "I'll go with you."

That was just what I wanted to hear.

CHAPTER 17

Carl and I were still sitting on the floor when Eleanor walked in. She called the police to report what Jack had done, but they said they couldn't do anything to him because he had not actually harmed me. They couldn't charge him with breaking and entering because the door had been unlocked. She was mad as a wet hen. She called Blake and asked him to bring her handgun when he came up for the weekend. Blake asked for Carl to get on the phone and tell him the whole story. I was still thinking about the handgun. I didn't even know my normally sweet, calm sister owned a handgun. She had never wanted anything to do with guns when we were kids. I was always the tomboy type and went hunting with Daddy, but somewhere along the line, Blake had convinced her to learn how to shoot one since he travelled most of the week and she needed to learn to protect herself.

The rest of the week went by in a blur. I was sicker than I had been through any of my chemo treatments and wanted nothing to eat. Eleanor force fed me crackers and ginger ale. Chuck had given me a bag of lemon drops to suck on when we first met. He said they helped him more than anything else with nausea when he went through chemo, and I found that they did help.

Carl came by to see me several times, but his explanations were still vague about what he was working on that made him disappear for days at a time.

"Cassie, just trust me. I wish I could tell you more, but the more you know, the more dangerous it would be for you."

"Is it dangerous for you?" I asked. "Because if it is.... Carl, are you involved in anything illegal?"

He laughed. "It depends on whose point of view you're looking at it from."

I put my fingers over my ears. "Don't tell me. I don't want to know."

"Just don't get upset with me if I don't tell you where I'm going."

I kept my fingers over my ears, but he pulled them off. "I promise that it will all be over soon, and then...."

"That doesn't help a bit," I said. "But I'll mind my own business."

"I just came by to tell you, I'll be leaving Friday and won't be back until next week. Your brother-in-law said he'd be here Friday morning, so I'll wait until then to leave." He smiled. "But I don't think you'll be having any more problems with Crum."

"You won't get to go to church with me." I said it as a fact instead of a question, disappointed none the less.

"I know, I'll make it up to you, I promise."

I got up from the couch. "Excuse me, I've got to go dry heave."

"Cassie," he said from behind me. I didn't turn around. I couldn't help that it irritated me to no end that he would tell me nothing. I wanted to be understanding, but I was too confused. When I came back from the bathroom, I was going to apologize, but he was gone.

By Friday, I was feeling much better, but I stayed inside anyway. He left in his boat before daylight. I knew, because I had set my alarm just so I could see him one more time. I watched him as he walked across the dock with his flashlight. As he stepped in his boat, I had a bad feeling that I couldn't shake and I lay there in my bed until I heard Eleanor get up. I put on my slippers and robe and drug myself to the kitchen to make coffee. I felt better physically, but my spirit was lagging behind. Blake would be coming in before lunch. Eleanor and I would both benefit from his evergoing optimism. It had been a stressful week, and just think, we would be repeating the chemo thing all over again on Monday. Grrr...

***

"Where's your neighbor tonight?" Blake asked as we ate the steak he had cooked. I guess I should say 'they' ate; I nibbled, but it felt good to finally feel like eating, even if it was only a small amount. That was the way it always happened. I could be sick to death one day, and feel halfway okay the next.

"He's gone for the weekend," I said, not volunteering any more information. I was afraid if I shared my suspicions, Blake would sweep us out of the house and back to the Lowcountry.

"That's a shame," he said. "I was hoping he'd be here so I could thank him again for coming to your rescue with the incident you had with the creep from the shrimp boat."

"Well, give me a little credit, too," I said. "I'm the one who came up with the bright idea of throwing up on him."

"That was fast thinking, Cassie. I brought Eleanor's gun and I want to teach you how to use it too, just in case something like this happens again."

"You forget who you're talking to, big bro. I was raised with a fishing pole in one hand and a shotgun in the other."

"But there's a difference in using a shotgun and a handgun," he said. "Have you ever used one?"

"That's true," I said. "When you shoot a shotgun, the shot scatters and your chances of hitting the target are a lot better. You have to take better aim with a rifle or handgun. But to answer your question, yes, I have a handgun in my safe back home and I've taken classes to learn how to use it."

"Good, I'll feel better knowing that you both know how to use one. I also feel better knowing that Carl is close by."

"He's gone a lot," Eleanor said.

"I know, he told me."

"He did?" I asked. I wondered what excuse he gave Blake about him being gone so much.

"Yeah, he seems like a nice guy. I'd like to get to know him better."

"Me too," I mumbled under my breath.

"What's that?" Blake asked.

"Oh, I just said yeah, he's a nice guy."

It turned out to be a good weekend with Blake. He and I went out in my little Jon boat and caught a few fish.

He was even nice enough to bait my hook since the shrimp were making me gag. Then he fried the fish up while Eleanor made French fries. I went to bed early on Saturday night so the two of them could have some time together. Eleanor seemed a little melancholy. I knew that they'd both be glad when things got back to normal and they could get on with their lives. Simon had said three more treatments and if that ended up not being enough, I would threaten to go live with him. That should do the trick. All thoughts of my dramatic intent on leaving the beach cottage to get even with Carl had been discarded.

On Sunday morning, I got up and took my shower early. I dressed in the new dress I had bought on our shopping trip in Wilmington, and took a bowl of cereal out to the gazebo to eat while watching the activity on the water. The parking area for boat trailers was full. Sunday was always a last minute rush for the weekenders to go out fishing one more time before they headed home. I heard Eleanor stirring around in the kitchen, then Blake stuck his head out the screen door.

"Do you want any breakfast?" he asked.

"No, I've already eaten some cereal."

"Good, that's what we'll eat. Don't have time for much of anything else before we go to church. We slept late." He closed the door and went back inside. I finished my coffee and took my empty cup and cereal bowl inside. They were still at the table eating. They both looked shocked when they saw me dressed for church.

I smiled at the look on their faces. "It's a long story," I said. "I'm going with you."

They exchanged glances but didn't ask any questions. "Well, let's get a move on girls. I'll be the envy of every man in there, walking in with a beautiful woman on each arm."

I just wished that Carl could be there. I loved my brother-in-law, but I would rather be walking in on Carl's arm. I had no misguided ideas about our relationship though. I had made up my mind that no matter how much I cared about him, I could never put up with his mysterious comings and goings. When I got back home, I would get over him, but those blue eyes would keep haunting me for the rest of my life and I knew I would never forget him. Did I really believe that? I was so fickle when it came to Mr. Blue Eyes. Each time he left, I thought I could get over him, but when he came back, wham, bam, I was head over heels again. If I was this confused myself, just think what I was doing to him, flip-flopping all over the place. He had been honest with me this last time, and I had gone off in a huff.

I had admired the little white clapboard church each time we passed by it. You could tell it was well loved by the condition it was in. A fresh coat of paint graced the outside and flowers were planted on each side of the sidewalk from the parking lot to the front door. Black iron railings were attached to brick steps that led up to the massive oak double doors. A bronze plaque was mounted on one side of the door saying it was built in 1921. It reminded me of other little churches built along the coastal regions of South Carolina.

The door was open and as we walked inside, a small elderly woman, not an inch over five feet tall and a man of about the same age and not much taller greeted us. In his younger years he would have been much taller, but he was bent over quite a bit, bless his heart. As they greeted us, they finished each other's sentences and I asked them if they were husband and wife. By the way the wife was smiling, I knew I'd guessed right.

"Yep, nigh on sixty years together," he said. "Only night we ever spent apart was when I was in the hospital last year."

"That's wonderful," Eleanor said. "What's your secret for being married so long?"

I thought the woman would answer, but she demurely looked at her husband. Seeing the twinkle in his eye, I was sure Eleanor had opened herself up for a good one.

"Well, it's like this," he said. "After we had three young'uns, we made a promise to each other."

"What was that?" Eleanor said. I love my sister but she can be so naive.

"We promised that the first one of us that got mad and packed up to leave had to pack up all the young'uns and take 'em with us."

We all laughed and the little woman puffed up with pride. It was easy to see she loved her man.

"I'm Wilbur Wainwright," the older man said, shaking our hands. "We're happy to have you with us and hope you enjoy your visit today."

With such a warm greeting, how could we not?

The inside of the church was just as warm and inviting as the outside. There was a center aisle with rows of richly polished pews on each side. In the alcove beyond the pulpit, a simple large white cross hung. I was filled with a deep longing for my life to be as it had been when I was a child. Blindly believing without a doubt. And as we heard the words of scripture read from the young man with a baritone voice, I had hope that it may come again. I went home and dusted off the books that Liz's husband, Rock had given me and I prayed my prayer.

CHAPTER 18

Monday and Tuesday seemed like a deja vous in Wilmington. Eleanor told Simon about how sick I was, so he called ahead for them to adjust the chemo formula and to also give me something for nausea. Miraculously my blood count was fine on Tuesday morning so they didn't need to give me a shot. My bones would be thankful and we made record time in getting back to the cottage. We pulled into the driveway a little before noon.

Carl's truck was still parked in the same position as it was when we left. I was anxious to tell him about church, but since he said he wouldn't be back until mid-week, I assumed he wasn't home. I could wait. I felt a renewal of spirit and found I was learning a little about patience. When we took our bags inside, I noticed that his boat was back at the dock, so apparently he was home after all. Eleanor and I took our lunch out on the gazebo to eat. All was quiet on the dock. All the shrimp boats were out and Gil had closed up the seafood house early, and was outside mowing with his push mower. We figured that since the trawlers hadn't made it back in yet, he had probably sold out of shrimp. No shrimp meant no customers. Other than Gil, there wasn't a soul in sight.

"This is the quietest I've seen this place all summer," Eleanor said.

"A lot of small boats have gone out today. Look at the parking lot." It was full of pickup trucks with boat trailers on the back - a lot more than normal for a weekday. "The fish must be biting. They'll come cruising back in here when their stomachs start rumbling for supper."

"Hey," she said, pointing to the dock, "what's wrong with Carl's boat?"

I looked down at his boat parked beside mine. Then I noticed mine was askew in the water with one of the ropes having come untied. His was tied with just one rope and the console windshield was broken and the cooler in the back was turned upside down.

"I wonder if he knows." Eleanor said.

"I'm sure he doesn't or he would be out here ranting and raving. I'll go tell him."

"I don't like the looks of this," Eleanor said. "I'll go with you."

We went down our set of steps to the dock below and walked over to his steps, climbing them in a hurry. I knocked hard but he didn't come to the door. We went around to the front of the house and knocked again. I looked into the kitchen window and it didn't look like anything had been disturbed. It was clean, just like he'd left it. We went around checking the windows and finally found one that wasn't locked.

"Give me a boost, Eleanor. I'm sure I can get in if I can just get a little push."

"Here, let me get the bench off the front porch, and you can climb up. I'm afraid I'll drop you. Maybe he's asleep."

"I don't think so," I said. "I knocked loud enough to wake the dead." Suddenly I felt a cold chill run up my spine. What if someone had come in and killed him. I hoped it was my writer's imagination, but I was frightened for him. And the last words I had spoken to him had been in anger. I wanted to take them back. "Pretty please, God", I whispered in a semi-silent prayer. "Don't let him be hurt."

Eleanor pulled the bench over to the window and I tried pushing the lower window up. The humidity at the beach makes doors and windows swell and this one was no exception, but I finally got it pushed up enough to crawl in. The room was his bedroom and the bed was made. I looked in the bathroom. His toothbrush was dry and the cap was on the toothpaste. The sink was spotlessly clean and the toilet lid was even down. If I hadn't been so worried, I would have smiled. How many men close the lid? Especially when they're alone. I walked through the rest of the house. All the lights were off except for a small lamp. I had seen the lamp on all the other times he had been gone overnight, so that wasn't unusual. I walked through the kitchen and opened the door to the outside.

"Well, is he in there?" she asked.

"No, and I don't like this at all. I think we should call the police." My suspicions were coming back. I wanted to believe in him, but... Maybe a drug deal had gone bad. I shuttered to think such a thing.

"Yes, definitely call the police," she said. As we were standing there talking, a black pickup truck came barreling into the driveway. There were two men and they opened the passenger and driver's side doors at the same time.

"Let's get out of here." I grabbed Eleanor's arm and pulled her along with me towards our house.

"Wait...please." I don't like commands from a man, but when it's followed by "please", we Southerners are too nice to turn away.

"And who are you?" I asked, trying to muster up bravado. Being nice doesn't mean we're weak.

"I'm Sean and this is Brent. We're friends of Carl's. Is he inside?"

"No, he isn't. How do I know you're his friends?

"We were here earlier this summer. We helped him move in."

Now I remembered where I had seen that black truck.

"We were just going to call the police. His boat is here, but it's a mess. Someone has broken the windshield and everything's topsy-turvy inside. His house is locked, but when he wouldn't come to the door, I went through an open window. It doesn't look like he's been here in days."

"And who are you?" the one named Sean asked.

"We're friends. We're staying in the cottage next door."

The two of them exchanged looks and smiled; then Sean spoke again. "So you're Cassie?"

"That's right. How do you know my name?" I don't know why, but I felt that my privacy had been invaded, but this wasn't the time to get in a conversation. "Never mind, just go look at his boat and see what you think. I'm afraid something's happened to him."

They went running down the steps to the dock and we followed right behind. They looked shocked when they saw the condition of the boat. Sean jumped in and looked through the papers in the dash while the other guy up-righted the cooler and checked the other compartments. He handed Sean a towel that was speckled with blood.

"Get the call in and be quick about it," Sean told his friend. "I don't like the looks of this." He turned to us. "You two go on back in your house and lock the doors. We'll take care of things from here."

"Aren't you going to call the police?" I asked. "I insist that you do, or I will." I was almost hysterical. "What about the water here - below the boat? Don't you think you need to look to make sure he hasn't ....?" I couldn't bring myself to say the word, drowned, but I was sick with worry.

"That's a good idea," Sean said. "We might find some clues. But, Cassie, try not to worry." He looked at me with concern. "I know it's foolish to tell you not to worry, but be assured, we'll make the call to the officials and you would be much better off inside. I promise to let you know as soon as I find out anything." Eleanor would later tell me that I was so pale, she thought I would faint right there on the dock.

Feeling defeated, I walked back up the steps hand in hand with Eleanor. Now, all we could do was wait for the police to arrive. Our unfinished lunch was on the table inside the gazebo with yellow jackets swarming around it. "Cassie, you go on inside. You're allergic to bee stings. I'll clean this up." Behind the screen door, I watched as she gathered up the plates and hurriedly carried them to the outside trash container with the yellow jackets following right behind. Why is it, I wondered, that the people who are not allergic never get stung. I fingered the epi-pen in my pocket. I take it with me everywhere I go, along with my lucky rabbit's foot. I don't believe in taking chances. It would be ironic to die of a bee sting after fighting cancer tooth-and-nail for the last few months.

"Cassie!" It was Eleanor calling me from the deck. I ran outside. "Look," she said, pointing to the boat dock. My boat was tied securely to the dock by both ropes. Carl's boat was speeding down the waterway with the guy named Brent behind the wheel. We both rushed out on the dock yelling at him, but he didn't turn around.

"I'll go to the front," Eleanor said. "You stay here."

"No way," I said, running after her. We stopped in our tracks when we saw the black truck was gone. Only Carl's truck remained behind.

"Oh my gosh," I said. "What have they done? And they seemed so nice." I sighed. "So much for nice, I'm calling the police like I should have done in the first place. I just know he's been kidnapped." I pulled out my phone. "Eleanor, how do you call 911 from cell phones? I've never had to do it before."

"Just go ahead and dial it," she said. "It should transmit our location and hook you up with the right dispatcher."

She was right and in just a few seconds, it was answered. "911, what is your situation?"

"There's been a kidnapping," I said. The stress of the moment finally hit me and I started hyperventilating.

"Ma'am, calm down. What's your location?"

I had to give the phone to Eleanor. I couldn't speak.

"What's that? Oh, yes - it's 12 Dolphin Lane, Lockwood Folly Landing. Please hurry."

He must have said something else because Eleanor said, "Yes, thank you," and ended the call.

"He said someone would be here within fifteen minutes." She hugged me as I stood there, not making a sound. "Cassie, they'll find out what happened. Please stop crying."

I pulled a tissue out of my pocket and blew my nose. "But now those guys have covered up all the evidence. They must be involved in it, somehow. They sure had me fooled!"

"They were strange guys, I must admit," she said. "But let's look at this logically. Maybe something busted his windshield out on the water. He could have run into something and injured himself and when he came back in, Gil or somebody else on the dock took him to the hospital. We don't know what happened. Why would you think he's been kidnapped?"

I looked up at her. How was I going to tell her about my suspicions that he was doing something illegal? I decided not to, because I didn't want to believe it myself, and because honest Eleanor would go blabbing it to the police. And besides, if she was right and he was just at a clinic or hospital, it wouldn't matter, would it. Otherwise, they would surmise he was a crook and not look for him.

"What else could I think, Eleanor? A busted up boat, a bloody towel - the whole scene looked like someone had scuffled around out there. And no sign of Carl. And it sure looks suspicious that those guys who said they were friends of Carl's just drove off after telling us they would call the police!"

"Wait up," she said. "Don't take it out on me."

"I'm sorry, I didn't mean to yell. I'm just so afraid he's hurt."

"Cassie, I know you two have become friends, but you don't know him that well. There's no sense in you taking this so hard."

"What?" I yelled. "You would take it hard too if something like this happened to Blake!"

She looked at me as if I had lost my mind. "That's different. Blake's my husband."

"Eleanor, haven't you guessed by now?" I paused. Maybe I had lost my mind. I sighed and shook my head. "I've only halfway admitted this to myself, but now I know. I'm in love with Carl."

She didn't even question me or look shocked, but instead wrapped her arms around me in her protective big-sisterly way. I think she had finally determined that nothing I said or did anymore could shock her. She must have thought I was going crazy, but she was taking it all in stride until I jumped back and scared her half to death.

"Eleanor! I forgot, I have his phone number! I can call him." She still had my phone and handed it to me. I scrolled through my contacts until I came to his name. It started ringing. "Please, God. Let him answer!" He didn't, but his voicemail did. I left a message.

***

Two men from the sheriff's department arrived twenty minutes later. One was a big, burly guy with a mustache and the other was a fresh faced kid. We told them everything we knew, including the part about the man who had sped off with Carl's boat, and his accomplice taking off in the black truck. They went down to the dock and looked around. The big guy came back to our deck while the other one looked inside my boat. He pulled at his chin and then rubbed along his mustache. It needed to be trimmed - the mustache, I mean. I hate bushy mustaches.

"Ma'am," he said, looking straight at me. I guess he figured I was the one who cared the most since my eyes were so red from crying. "There's no evidence at all down there, but I'm going to take your word for it. May we look inside the house?"

"Sure," Eleanor said. "My sister left the front door open when she came out after looking for him inside."

"Did you tamper with anything? Leave any fingerprints?"

"No," I said. "Only on the window when I opened it, and on the door knob when I opened it from inside and closed it back from outside. I've tried calling his cell number and he doesn't answer."

He looked at me carefully. "And what is your relationship with the man who's missing?"

I didn't know what to say. What exactly was our relationship? We hadn't really talked about a relationship...yet.

"He's just a good friend," Eleanor said, looking at me, then back at the deputy.

"What does he do?"

I looked confused.

"I mean, where does he work?"

Again, I didn't know what to say. Should I just say, I don't know - he hasn't told me? Didn't really good friends tell those kinds of things to each other?

"I don't really know," I said. "We just met about a month ago and all I know is that he's on vacation. We really didn't talk about our jobs."

"And what do you do?" he asked, looking at me suspiciously. Why was he asking me that? It really wasn't his business.

"She's a writer," Eleanor said. "And she's my sister," she said possessively. "She's also recuperating from a chemo treatment she had just yesterday, so she's under a lot of stress. We've told you all we know. Just find him, please."

He looked properly chastised. Thank you Eleanor! I said it with my eyes as she looked worriedly at me to see how I was holding up. I was so glad she was taking charge. All I wanted to do was cry.

After about fifteen minutes they came out of the house with some papers. I couldn't tell what they were, but at least they didn't have his book about drug smuggling. I didn't want them to get any ideas.

"We found a copy of his boat registration," Mr. Mustache said. "We'll check the nearby hospitals first. If he's not there, we'll put out an all-points bulletin with the Coast Guard to be on the lookout for his boat. Don't worry, ma'am, we'll find him."

Somehow I didn't feel very confident as they casually shuffled back to the squad car. I took my trusty rabbit's foot out of my pocket and rubbed back and forth. The tufts of fur had worn off over the years, but my

Lowcountry upbringing, running through the marshy forests with my childhood friend, Mingo Baker, had instilled in me some of the Gullah superstitions and traditions. He would show me his ancestor's graves marked only by a stone or rock, buried near the waterfront because they believed that spirits can move across the water. He was the one who had given me my rabbit's foot, telling me that whatever I did, to always hold on to it for luck. He said a real rabbit had paid the price and died so as I could have good luck. I think he was getting it mixed up with Jesus. I had asked him how come the rabbit had blue fur and he said those were the best kinds for luck. I looked at it now and wondered if he had given me a green one, would my luck have been better.

Eleanor looked down at my hand. She wrinkled up her nose. "Cassie," she said. "Do you still have that disgusting thing? Surely you know that it isn't real!"

"Yes it is! Mingo Baker gave it to me years ago."

"Cassie, every dime store in Charleston County sold those things for ten cents apiece. They were made in Japan."

I looked at it carefully. I had always wondered why it didn't have little claws. "Dang it," I said. "So that's why my luck has been so lousy all these years. I've been rubbing on a fake rabbit's foot." I drew my arm back and gave it a fling towards the water. It landed with a plop and a seagull sitting on one of the pilings swooped down and got it. He carried it about twenty feet over the water and then dropped it in mid-flight. I guess he found it disgusting too.

"Luck and superstition don't have anything to do with it," Eleanor said. "If you want to do something productive, we'll sit down here on the steps and pray that Carl is safe." She looked up at me with her kind eyes. "Did you know I pray for you every day, Cassie?"

"Carl said the same thing when we went to Bird Island. Apparently that's not doing any good either, but what have we got to lose?"

Eleanor has such a sweet, clear voice. I kind of envy her the way she carries on, talking to God. You would think he's her best friend or something. I didn't tell her I had prayed the big prayer. I was still sorting out things and I had a long way to go.

CHAPTER 19

Carl:

They must have been in the cabin cruiser waiting for me. It was parked three slips down from mine and I noticed it when I rounded the corner of the inlet. I hadn't seen it docked there before, but boats were always coming in and out of the docks to buy shrimp and fish from the fish houses. Still, I should have paid more attention. It's hard to pay attention to details when you've got more than work on your mind. I'm usually more careful, but I was distracted trying to see if Cassie had made it back from Wilmington.

Women! I knew better, but those green eyes were haunting me day and night. It was bad enough having the dangers of the job to worry about, but now I worried about her too. What if the chemo didn't work? What if Jack Crum came back and tried to harm her? I had let my heart rule rather than my head, and by letting my guard down, here I was in a position that I couldn't help her at all.

I was securing my boat to the dock when they slipped up behind me. I barely had time to react. I managed to jump in the boat, but I couldn't get the key in the ignition fast enough to get away. They were on top of me before I could do anything about it. At least I got in a few good hits, one of them probably has a broken nose, or at least it was gushing blood from the sharp jab I made with my elbow. But then there was a dull thud, a sharp pain over my left ear, and I was out. I slipped in and out of consciousness long enough to know that I was at one time lying in the berth of the boat amidst life jackets and oars and there was a strong smell of engine oil. I was covered with a blue tarp, but enough light was filtering through it for me to see. The choppy seas produced a jolt with each wave we hit and my head felt as if it would explode along with the contents of my stomach.

I tried to keep track of the time we were on the small boat, but I don't know how much of the trip I was conscious. If I had to guess, I would say less than an hour's time passed before they wrapped me up in the tarp and hoisted me up like dead weight in something that felt like a large seine or net onto the floor of a ship. Their voices sounded muffled to my pounding head, but from their conversations, I knew that one's name was Harvey; the smallest one. If I had been fighting two the size of Harvey, they wouldn't have cornered me. But I was no match for the big one.

Next they lowered me down into the cargo area with the tarp, and dropped me the rest of the way. I fell with the tarp still wrapped halfway around me, jarring my head and body on the wood floor below. The sound of the hatch closing and the darkness that followed confirmed my worst fears. I felt like a prisoner must feel when he's being held without bond and he hears those prison doors slam shut and lock. But at least prisoners can see. I was blind as a bat, and I'm the worst of the worst claustrophobics.

I shifted positions, hoping to feel my cell phone holder still attached to my belt. No such luck. Even my belt was gone, along with my wallet, all undoubtedly dumped into the sea by now. If they were smart, they would have dumped my cell phone first to keep it from transmitting a location signal. There was nothing to identify me in my wallet except my driver's license with a fake name and some "family" pictures of a family that didn't exist. Did they know who I was? If they had, I would most likely be at the bottom of the sea. Most of the drug lords responsible for importing by sea have no problems making a person disappear without a trace. The sea is an unforgiving crime scene where sharks are well known for getting rid of evidence.

Wiggling my way out of the tarp, I saw a thin line of light above me, a slight crack in the hatch door. Where there's light, there is hope. I thought of the scripture, John 8:12. Jesus had gone up to the Mount of Olives and was teaching in the temple court. He said to them, "I am the Light of the world; he who follows Me will not walk in the darkness, but will have the Light of life." My faith walk hasn't been perfect, but I've never doubted that He is the light. At that time, Jesus' hour had not come. My hope was that mine hadn't either. I needed to be strong. I have a strong desire to live, for there's justice that needs to be done and there's a beautiful, witty, strong-willed woman who's fighting a battle too big for her to bear and I want to be there to help her figure it all out.

I wiggled my hands. I could tell the ropes were nylon, the same type I have on the boat and a little easier to unknot than cotton or silk. At least my feet weren't bound. I tried to stand up. My head pounded and I sank back to the floor, but after a few more attempts, using the wall to brace myself, I made it. I paced the length, then the width, figuring it to be about a ten by eighteen foot storage area.

My eyes slowly adjusted to the small slivers of light coming from the hatch door and I could tell I was in the ship's pantry hold where food is normally stored, but the only telltale evidence that it was once a pantry was an old apple or orange crate and a grain barrel which I felt rather than saw with so little light available.

From the thin line of light, I tried to gauge the height. Based on my knowledge of ships of the same size, it shouldn't be over ten feet high. Even if I got my hands free, there was no way I could get myself up that high. There was usually a ladder from the hatch to the floor, but it had been conveniently, or inconveniently for me, relocated. The area was completely empty, nothing at all to stand on except maybe the barrel. Next, I checked the walls, brushing up against them to see if anything caught on my clothes. Sometimes these ships had hooks for hanging salt cured meats, but no such luck. But then again, I could only check as high as my shoulder. It was time to start working on loosening the ropes.

Suddenly I heard voices up ahead, and the hatch door was being lifted. I slammed myself back on the floor and wriggled under the tarp the best I could before it opened completely. A bright beam of light scattered about on the floor around me until it came to rest where I was settled under the tarp.

"Is he still alive?" It was the voice I had heard somewhere before, but I still couldn't place it.

"I don't know. He was still breathing when we put him down there but he hasn't moved. I guess you bumped him on the head pretty good. I'll throw the bottle of water down there. He'll be needing it."

There was a loud laugh from the other one. "Not if he's dead, and if he ain't dead, he's going to wish he was when the Captain gets through with him."

Captain? Dirty Jack must be involved. The beam of the light went out. Without it, they couldn't see into the dark hole where I was lying. I could still see the light from the opening of the hatch door and I quickly pulled my head from under the tarp. There it was, the prettiest sight I could have hoped to see. Hooks lined the wall about eight feet up. I didn't know how I was going to get to them, but it gave me hope. And having hope makes all the difference.

The hatch door slammed loudly but I didn't hear the lock click in place. Suddenly I was thirsty, a trick of the mind because there was water and I couldn't get it with my hands tied. The thirst gave me an even greater incentive to get out of the ropes. As I moved around, I felt something wet and slippery on one side of the tarp. Motor oil; apparently what I smelled in the berth of the cabin cruiser and the tarp had absorbed some of it. I soaked my wrists in the oil and finally, by stretching the rope out, my right hand came free. I groped for the water bottle, opened it and took a few sips, rationing it since I didn't know how long I would be there. The movement had made my head start pounding again and I tried to rest on the cold hard floor. I would need my strength for later.

Eleanor:

To tell you the truth, I was terribly frightened after the shock of Carl's disappearance wore off. I wanted to take Cassie and go back home, but she insisted on staying.

"Go on home, Eleanor," she said. "I can't leave until I find out what's happened to Carl."

I called Blake and he assured me he would leave immediately to come up. Too many things had happened; the incident with Jack Crum should have been a warning to go home, but at the time, Blake and I both thought it was an isolated event. With Carl's strange disappearance, I no longer felt safe at all. The beautiful, peaceful place that had once seemed like an oasis was beginning to feel like a nightmare. I kept hoping that perhaps Carl had decided to go with someone else on a boat ride, and his boat was vandalized after he left. When I voiced that thought to Cassie, she accused me of being ever the optimist. I suppose I am an optimist, but it's my opinion that if you're always expecting doom and gloom, it's bound to happen. The only logical thing to do was to get down on my knees and pray for a miracle.

I was floored when Cassie expressed her strong feelings for Carl. She'd certainly kept those feelings to herself, even acting rather put out with him at times, but Cassie has never been one to wear her heart on her sleeve. He'd been very attentive of her after her last chemo and after the incident with Jack, but still, she always seemed a little distant with him. Maybe that's her way of handling her emotions. She has such a tough exterior and I keep forgetting how vulnerable she really is.

It's funny how news travels. The dock had been so quiet when we first got home from Wilmington, but then it became all a'buzz with a possible kidnapping, some even going so far as to speculate a murder. After Cassie heard that one, she went into the house and curled up on the sofa with a comforter over her head. I would feel safer when Blake arrived, but, like Gil at the fish house said, nothing else would happen with all eyes on the waterway.

CHAPTER 20

I finally decided that hiding under a blanket on the sofa wouldn't accomplish anything. I needed some plan of action.

The dock was full of people, most of them gathered around Wenona's. Eleanor seemed surprised to see me outside.

"I'm going back inside Carl's house," I said.

"Do you think you should? I mean, isn't it considered a crime scene or something?"

"Of course not. The police checked it and nothing seemed out of place. I just want to see if I can find something...., anything that may give us an idea of who could have wanted to harm Carl. Maybe there'll be a little black book or something."

She looked at me skeptically. "You've been reading too many who-done-it books. People don't have little black books anymore. They keep their contacts in their cell phones."

"I have a little black book. I would be lost without it," I said. "And I'll bet you do too." I gave her the stare down.

"I do, but we're the exception."

"It doesn't matter. I'm going in there."

She rolled her eyes. "Well, I guess it wouldn't do any good to try to dissuade you. You've got your mind made up. Do you think the policemen left the door open?"

"If not, I'll crawl in the bedroom window again. They couldn't have locked it - the lock's broken."

"Why don't you wait until Blake comes?" She took one look at my stubborn set jaw and just shook her head. "Oh, go ahead. If anyone gets nosy, I'll make up something to tell them."

I walked around the house so that I could try the front door, the one I left open when Carl's friends had showed up. Some friends they were, running off with the evidence. I tried the door. It was locked. The window was still wide open and the bench hadn't been moved. Looking around to make sure no one was looking, I hefted myself through and was inside in a matter of seconds.

I sat on the side of his bed. Thinking the nightstand would be a good place to start looking for his address book, I opened the drawer. There was a small notepad and pen inside, along with three books. I picked each one up and thumbed through the pages, wondering if he had hidden any notes inside. An odd combination of books, I thought: *The Bible*; *Man Riding West* by Louis L'Amour; and the book I had seen earlier on the coffee table, *Drug Smuggling along the Atlantic Coast*, by Carlton Wright. It was the last book to thumb through and as I did, a single sheet of paper fell out. It looked like some random letters and numbers, two lines of them, or maybe it was a formula. I looked at them carefully. The first line was "LAN32 46 7.7918 and the second was LOW78 5.5 32.8125. LAN? Wasn't that some sort of file server on a computer? I had heard of it before. I racked my brain trying to dig back into my computer knowledge, oh yeah, Local Area Network is what it stands for. But what could LOW mean. I knew he had a laptop. It could still be inside the house since I didn't see the police leave with it. I stuck the paper back in the book and put it on top of the nightstand to take with me. I wondered if it could be a secret code of something. Lord have mercy - last week I would have laughed at secret codes and formulas, but with the onset of the strange happenings, I wouldn't discount anything. Maybe the book at least would give me some insight into the kind of people Carl was dealing with. The bed creaked a little as I shifted my position. It was neatly made up with a sailboat themed comforter, and the matching pillow sham was fluffed up atop his pillow. I lifted his pillow from under the sham and held it up to my face. It smelled of his aftershave lotion and I buried my face in it, remembering too vividly the last kiss we shared. The night of the fabulous sunset; the night I had the first inkling I was in love with him. I breathed in and out a few times, and I swear, my heart hurt just thinking about him. It was a feel good hurt, not a heartbreak kind of hurt, but it made me miss him and worry about him.

"Enough daydreaming, Cassie," I said, under my breath, but it sounded loud in the empty house. It gave me an eerie feeling, and then an even eerier feeling when I heard a loud crash in the kitchen. I froze in place. Oh my gosh, someone was in the house. I came to my senses and grabbed the book. I thought about climbing back out the window, but it was awkward getting in and out, and Lord knows, I didn't want to be halfway out and have someone pull me back in. I ran for the bathroom instead, pulling the door partially closed behind me, then changing my mind, I pulled it open slightly. A closed door draws more attention than an open door and if they heard me, hopefully they would think I made it out the window. I got in the bathtub and hid behind the shower curtain. I felt, rather than heard a presence in the bedroom.

Please go away, please, please, I thought to myself as if I could wish the person away. But no such luck. I had thrown away my rabbit's foot too soon. I heard the creak of the door as it opened inward. I picked up a bottle of shampoo from the corner of the tub. If I could squeeze soap in his eyes....Then, quick as a flash, the shower curtain, rod and all came crashing in on me, leaving me flailing around with the curtain on top of my head. I screamed, but my scream was muffled with plastic all around me.

CHAPTER 21

"Stupid cat, stupid, stupid cat!" Raphael was purring and wrapping himself around my legs as I was extricating myself from the plastic. He had sensed my presence just as I had sensed his, and undoubtedly saw a slight movement or my shadow behind the shower curtain, thus the pounce of a lifetime that seriously almost gave me a heart attack. "You just had to be nosy and come through the open window, didn't you?" I asked him. "Didn't you ever hear that curiosity killed the cat? Or does it amuse you to scare the living crap out of me?" He just looked at me and started wrapping his body around my legs again.

"Cassie?" It was Blake's voice coming from outside the window. "Who are you talking to?" He sounded alarmed.

"It's Raphael," I said, finally free and crawling out of the bathtub. "He didn't think I'd had enough excitement for the day." I walked in the bedroom and to the window.

"I don't think you should be in there," he said. "What if the police come back?"

"I told them Carl and I are friends. I'll tell them we go in and out of each other's houses, which is true, sort of." I had finally made my way to the window. "I'll run around and open the door for you," I said.

"No, I think you should come out." His voice was firm.

"Okay-y-y!" I said. "I've got to clean up whatever mess the cat made in the kitchen first. He crashed something all over the floor. At least come in and help me clean up."

"Alright, open the door then, but we need to do it quickly and get out of here."

Raphael continued to bug us as Blake and I picked up broken shards of a coffee cup and several pieces of silverware from the floor. He had jumped on the counter and knocked over the dish drainer, scattering things everywhere. Blake got the broom and started sweeping up the remaining pieces of broken pottery while I made a quick run-through of the rest of the house. I spotted the laptop. It was in its satchel pushed up under the tiny desk in the corner of the living room. I handed it to Blake along with the book I had taken and went back to the bedroom. Raphael was sitting on the windowsill looking out. I pushed him out and closed the window. It wouldn't lock, but I picked up a small wooden bowl filled with loose change and sat it so that if the window was opened from the outside, the bowl would fall off, hopefully scaring away any burglar who happened to be looking for an easy break-in. There was a spare key hanging from a nail just inside the kitchen door, so I took it, just in case we needed to get back in.

"Oh, wait a minute," I said to Blake as he started out the door. "I forgot something." I ran back into the bedroom and grabbed Carl's pillow. It would be a long night and I needed the pillow to comfort me.

***

Blake had been on the phone for the last hour while I had been trying to take a nap. My energy level had crashed, but sleep eluded me. I felt in my bones that Carl was in real trouble and there was nothing we could do. I walked back into the living room and he had just plugged in the computer. He looked up as I walked in.

"You couldn't sleep?"

"No. I'm worried, Blake."

"Cassie, I can't believe that I left you two alone here with someone that we barely know. I really trusted him too. He was so concerned about you, even calling me to find out the results of your scan the last time we were in Charlotte. I have his cell phone number and I've been calling him, but he doesn't answer."

"Me too. I've tried several times now. It just goes to voicemail."

"After I first met him, I wanted to be sure he was an okay guy, so I looked him up on the internet and even found out where he works, or so I thought."

"What? You didn't tell me. I should have thought of that! What did you find out?"

Eleanor brought in some iced tea and set it on the table.

"I found a Carl McGee in Wilmington. He's a contractor and had glowing reports from happy homeowners on the Better Business Bureau's site. I guess I didn't dig deep enough."

"What do you mean?" Eleanor said.

"I just now called the man's house number and his wife answered."

I felt the color drain from my face. "His wife?"

"Yes, and she said he was at the office, so I called the office and his secretary answered. She said he had just left five minutes ago. I asked her if he had been in all day and that I thought he was on vacation.

I was dreading to hear the answer. "And..."

"The secretary laughed and said that he never takes a vacation. He hasn't missed a day of work since she starting working for him over two years ago."

Eleanor looked up at me. "So it can't be our Carl?" she said.

"No, and now I'm beginning to wonder what his name really is." By that time the laptop had finished booting up and was asking for a password. "Great!" Blake's shoulders dropped and he banged his fist on the coffee table. "The mystery man has a password, and we won't be able to guess it in a thousand years."

I thought about the note paper that was inside the book from Carl's nightstand. "Wait a minute," I said, "I found a piece of paper in the book I gave you to bring over here. Maybe he thought it was a safe place for a password." I thought about the long row of numbers and letters. "It's an awfully long password though, if that's what it is."

Blake looked hopeful. "It can't hurt to try. Where is it?"

"I put it in Cassie's bedroom," Eleanor said.

I walked to my bedroom and took the paper out of the book. "Here it is," I said, walking back to Blake and the laptop. I handed it to him.

"It is long," he said. "We'll try the top row first." He looked at it carefully. "There's some spaces in between. I don't think you can have spaces in passwords, but I'll try. It's the best we've got." He input the letters and numbers and I watched as something came up on the screen. *Incorrect password. Try again.*

"Maybe it's just the first few letters before the space." He tried it and the same message came up. He studied the numbers carefully and then jumped up.

"Cassie, do you know what this is?"

"No, it didn't make any sense to me. I thought it had something to do with computers because of the LAN letters at the beginning."

"Look at this!" He held his finger over the letters *LA* and pointed to the rest.

I read them aloud, "N32 46 7.7918"

"And now read the second row with me covering the first two letters."

"W78 5.5 32.8125." I looked at him excitedly. "Blake, they're map coordinates. Oceanography coordinates! And the *LA* stand for latitude and *LO* for longitude. And the *N* and *W* are North and West. I didn't notice it because the letters were all running together." I looked between him and Eleanor. "Do you think it's a clue?"

"I don't know, but maybe we can find out if we get this computer going. I'll go online and see if the coordinates are in this area." He stared at me for a moment. "Cassie, you know Carl much better than I do. Could you take a guess at a password he might use?"

I thought for a minute. I knew his daughter's name was Carly. Or did I? If his name wasn't Carl McGee, he had probably lied about his daughter too.

"Here, let me try. Where are my reading glasses, Eleanor?"

"Probably in your bedroom. I'll go see."

She came back with the glasses. I kneeled down at the table and turned the laptop facing me. I typed in his daughter's name; the brand and make of his truck; then his boat, but each time it turned up the same message: *Incorrect password. Try again.* Frustrated, I typed in my own name and did a double take when the password screen disappeared and a Microsoft page pulled up.

"You guessed it! What was it?" Blake asked.

I blushed, then smiled and looked up at him over my glasses. "It was my name."

The smile left his face. "Cassie, Eleanor tells me that you think you're in love with Carl."

I could tell that he didn't approve and my rebel spirit came through. "Yes, I am," I said defiantly, "and it's obvious he feels something for me. He used my name for his password. Doesn't that prove something?"

He sighed. "I'll admit that it does, but you don't even know him, Cassie."

He had me there, and I hung my head for a minute. Then I remembered Carl's eyes and his sweet spirit and I looked back up hoping Blake would understand. "But I do know him. No matter what he is or isn't, I know that he's a good and decent man. You're right, though.

There's something he's not telling me, but he promised to explain it all soon. I love him, Blake, and I know he loves me too."

He smiled gently and put his arm around my shoulder. "If he means that much to you, I'm going to find him, come hell or high water. You do have a way of picking complicated men, though. Why can't you fall for a car mechanic or a computer programmer?"

"Well, we do know what he's not," I said.

"What's that?"

"Carl McGee, the contractor."

It was the only allusion to humor in any of our discussions all afternoon, and we all laughed. It relieved a little of the stress. Luckily, the WiFi at Wenona's Place didn't require a password and Blake was able to pull up the coordinates from the piece of paper.

"It's about twelve miles offshore," he said. "I'm calling the Coast Guard."

CHAPTER 22

Carl:

I forced myself up off the floor. While lying there I had thought of a plan of action. I pushed the three foot tall grain barrel underneath the hatch door and put the apple crate on top of it. I would be able to reach the hatch door if I stood on both, but I wouldn't have any leverage to open it. My best bet was to fasten the tarp to the hooks on each side of the walls and try to form a hammock of sorts. It would take a balancing act that I wasn't sure I had in me to stand up on it, but it was the only chance I had. I pulled the tarp up into a large heap so that when I climbed up on the barrel, I could reach down and pick it up. When I climbed upon the barrel, I found I could reach the hooks without having to stand on the apple crate, but it could possibly come in handy so I reached up and hung it on one of the hooks. I carefully started threading the tarp's metal reinforced rings on the hooks until I had three on each side. Now it was time to test it. I used my upper body strength to hoist myself up from the barrel onto my newly made hammock, but I overestimated the amount of push I would need and flipped over the tarp, almost knocking the barrel down in the process. I still had a good grip on the tarp and steadied the barrel, giving it another try. This time I was successful and lay in the hammock until I could bring myself to stand up.

I lay there for a moment having to force myself to stay alert. The knock on my head had taken its toll.

I thought of Cassie and wondered if she even knew I was gone. Would she be worrying about me? I wondered how her treatment in Wilmington had gone and hoped she wouldn't be so sick like she had been the week before. She and Eleanor should have been home shortly after I was attacked. Hoping to see how she had fared was the only reason I had gone back to the dock. I should have met Brent and Sean at the rendezvous point like we had planned instead of going back. That's why it's been drilled into us that there's safety in numbers. But at least they would be looking for me. When I didn't show up and they couldn't reach me by phone, it would throw up a red flag because they knew how close I was to making the bust.

Surely they would come looking for me, wouldn't they? And would they remember the coordinates I had given them. My source had been sure that was where the ship would be headed.

"Face it, Carl, you're in trouble." I don't pray as often as I should, but like most people, when I'm in trouble, I pray, and that's just what I did. For Cassie; for someone to be looking for me; and for me to have the strength for whatever lay ahead.

When I finished my prayer, I tried to stand up. It was harder than I thought. I reached over and grabbed the apple crate from the hook and nestled it down in the tarp. Maybe it would give me a better foothold. It seemed to be working, so I slowly stood up holding both hands against the side of the wall near the hatch door. I reached up to touch it and found that it had worked. I should be able to push it fully open if I could stay balanced on the tarp.

Just as I started to push, I heard footsteps overhead. I heard the sound of something dropping beside the hatch and then it began to lift open. I saw one set of feet before it opened all the way.

"Hey down there, pretty boy. I've been sent by the captain to feed you, and I have no idea why. If I had my way, you'd rot down there. It ain't no picnic - just a banana and a can of Beanie Weenies, but it'll keep you alive. If you don't want your head bashed in any more, you better get to the left while I throw down the can. For some reason, the captain don't want you dead."

It was the one called Harvey, and before he could turn on the flashlight, I grabbed for his feet. It caught him off guard and before he could make a noise other than a grunt, I had pulled him by both feet into the opening. As I pulled, I pushed him to the side and down so he wouldn't hit the tarp that I was standing on. If he did, we'd both fall off. He fell to the floor with a thud. The momentum almost made me lose my balance and I was in danger of falling with him, but I managed to keep my grip on the tarp. When I had settled back on the sling, I looked down. He wasn't making a sound, so apparently he'd been knocked out. I hoped he was still alive, although he seemed to have earlier not cared one way or the other about me.

The door was open and waiting for me. With a new resolve, I gripped the edge of the opening and hoisted myself up. I swiftly closed the hatch door and latched it, then moving quickly, I ran for cover. I was on the bottom deck and I ducked under the stairwell to gather my thoughts and decide what to do next. I wondered how many people were on the ship. Frank Osborne, a rogue shrimp boat captain had been under suspicion during our whole operation. He had spent time in jail for smuggling, and it was rumored that he was up to his old habits. But when Crum showed up out of the blue, we began to focus on him as well. Both are bad dudes. I suddenly wished for a weapon, any kind of weapon.

I looked around for a better place to hide, but nothing provided any better protection than under the stairs. I tried to slide back a little farther but a big metal box was in my way. I felt around it and discovered it had a door that opened from the top. I lifted the lid. All I saw were life rings, several of them, but then I felt around underneath the rings and found a rope ladder, the kind you drop for people to board your boat. It was something I would need if I managed to find a way to escape.

I had happened upon their emergency box and I had been lucky to find it. Feeling around a little more, I found what I was hoping for. It was an orange plastic box just like those we're issued on our boats. Hallelujah! I knew what was inside and I wasn't disappointed when I opened it to find a twelve gage flare gun with extra flares and about six handheld flares. I had found my weapon and I felt that same sense of hope that I had felt earlier when I saw those hooks. Hope and faith - two things that buoy you and give you the courage to face whatever happens. They've gotten me out of many difficult situations, and I prayed once more that they would this time.

Now for some action - I knew I needed to prepare before someone came looking for poor Harv, bless his soul. I looked around the corner and didn't see anyone coming. I took the rope ladder and ran to the rails on the side of the ship that I didn't think they would use since the deck was covered in huge shipping crates. I threw the ladder down the side between two of the posts and tied the ends to the bottom of the rails. I had done this many times before during rescues. I stood back and looked and the ladder wasn't obvious at all from the deck. Someone could walk right by it and never notice. I ran back under the stairwell and grabbed the flare gun. I would be ready when they came. I could at least get one of them with the flare gun and I knew who I would aim for, the big one. I sat down on the box to wait. Looking up at the sky, I whispered, "Thank you, God, for showing up when I needed you. Give me the strength I need to finish the job. Amen." Short and sweet, but I knew He listened.

I heard voices coming down the stairs and pushed myself as far back as I could. My ears were still ringing from the blow to my head, but I could make out what they were saying. I hoped they didn't discover me, because I could only get one of them with the flare gun, and I still wasn't confident that the dizziness I had been feeling would allow me to take on the other one. Luckily they didn't come around to the side of the stairwell, but went to the left instead.

"I wonder where Harvey ran off to. He was supposed to throw the food down and come right back." It was the big guy. I heard the other one mutter, but couldn't understand what he said. The big guy did though, because he laughed. "I wouldn't doubt it. He's probably drunk as a skunk. He's got a hidden stash of whiskey somewhere, so he's more'n likely passed out in his bunk."

Then the other one answered and this time I heard him loud and clear.

"Probably so. I'm takin' the shrimp boat back out. When I've had time to get away, move the ship further out to sea to the coordinates I left in the cabin. That's the rendezvous point to get rid of these last crates. A trawler named Iron Gate will pick them up. I'll be glad when we get this over with. When you leave there, put the dinghy out and set your tourist adrift in it. It'll take a while for anyone to find him from out there."

"Why not let us just dump him overboard?"

"No! I don't want anyone dead. Roughing him up like that was bad enough, but I guess it was necessary to give us time. Given more time, he could have blown the whistle on our location just by being in the wrong place at the wrong time." He paused. I was afraid for a moment that I had made a noise and they heard me, but then he started talking again.

"Are you sure that you covered your tracks when you picked him up? I still think you should have taken his boat. People will wonder why it's parked at the dock and he's not there."

"We left everything just as it should be. No signs at all that we were there."

I knew that was a lie. They couldn't have had time to clean up the mess they made of my boat. I guess he just didn't want to admit he'd been clumsy.

"Okay, then... I'll radio you later this evening so you and Nate can get the ship on back to Florida. Harvey won't be much help if he's drunk. This is going to be my first and last run. Nothing else illegal for me. You've got your share of the money, and if you do what I've said, I'll wire you a bonus when you get back to Florida."

Oh my gosh! I knew that voice. And he was leaving. Now I was more worried than ever about Cassie. But thank God, he wasn't planning to kill me after all.

I stayed where I was and heard the sound of the shrimp boat when the engines turned. So there was one other person on board who hadn't shown himself yet - Nate. I listened as the noise of the engine grew fainter. Footsteps sounded again, first on the deck and then starting up the first steps. Then I heard the big guy's voice mumbling as he made his way up the stairs and what I heard sent chills up my spine.

"Bonus, be damned. That man'll be shark bait before we leave for Florida. I'm not having him around to identify me."

CHAPTER 23

I was beside myself while Blake was on the phone with the Coast Guard. Hurry, I wanted to yell at them, but Blake explained it well, without getting flustered like I would have done. When he got off, he looked puzzled.

"What?" I asked him. "What did they say?"

"They said they'd already been called. They're looking for him now. But they were glad to get the coordinates - said it would narrow their search. I wonder if the police called them."

"Or maybe it was those two guys who called, you know, the ones who said they were Carl's friends, Brent and Sean. And here I was, thinking they'd stolen Carl's boat."

I was biting on my fingers, just like I've done since I was a kid. Momma told me it would make ugly calluses on my hands. Daddy just told me that calluses never hurt anybody. "It'll keep a fish hook from going through your skin," he would say. "Keep on biting." Then he would rub his hand over the top of my head. I always knew I was his favorite. He's been gone nigh on five years now, barely lived six months after Momma died, both from cancer. I guess I got their cancer genes. I still miss them. Growing up on the water was always my saving grace as a child. I was the poet and ponderer in the family and being in our little family boat all by myself had been instrumental in keeping my sanity.

"I think I'll take the boat out for a ride to clear my head."

"Cassie, please don't," Eleanor said. "I don't think it's safe for you to go out alone. Jack Crum is out there somewhere. Who knows, he may be responsible for what's happened to Carl. Maybe he's trying to get even with him for being so protective of you after the incident here at the house."

I truly had not thought of that and it gave me a sickening feeling.

"That's right, Cassie," Blake said. "But if you're set on going out for a while, I'll go with you. Being on the water always calms you, and I promise I'll just go along for the ride and be silent for a change."

"Ha," I said. "I want to see that. I've never seen you be quiet long enough to sneeze."

He laughed. "Well, get the boat keys. You can time me." He turned to Eleanor with a look of concern. "Will you be okay here by yourself?"

"Sure, this place is crawling with people now, waiting to see what happens. I'll just sit on the gazebo. With all the people around, I'll be fine. Besides, I saw Captain Chuck pull his shrimp boat up to the dock when I came back in here from making the tea. He'll watch after me."

"He's here?" I jumped up and ran to the window. We hadn't opened up the blinds since we got home, and I pulled them open so I could see the dock at Wenona's Place. "He is here! I'm going down to talk to him. Do y'all want to come with me?"

"I'll stay here," Eleanor said. "Blake, you go ahead. Just keep your cell phones handy."

"That's not all I'm keeping handy." He walked back to Eleanor's bedroom and returned wearing a blue lightweight sailing jacket. "For the boat ride," he said. "Cassie, you should get your jacket too in case it gets cool on the water." Before he zipped it, I noticed a bulge under his left arm, and knew that he was carrying his concealed carry revolver. It made me feel safer, knowing he had it handy.

"Aye, aye, Captain," I said, and walked to the tiny coat closet to retrieve my jacket. While they were talking, I took the paper with the map coordinates off the table and stuffed it into my jacket pocket.

When Blake and I got down to the dock, Chuck was still tying off the ropes. I went to see if could help.

"Cassie, you're a sight for sore eyes. I was wondering if you would be here when I got back." He stopped what he was doing and gave me a bear hug.

"I'm glad you're here." I looked around and didn't see Johnny or Red. "Where's your help?" I asked.

"I didn't take 'em with me this time. I've just been out scouting some new places to shrimp. Our honey hole has dried up. The water's getting hotter so we're gonna have to go further up the shore if we're going to get what we need. Maybe on up towards the Pamlico Sound."

He took the last rope from me and tied it off. "How are you doing, Cassie? Chemo still making you sick?"

"Not as bad this time."

Blake had made his way up to where we were standing. "Where are my manners," I said. "Blake, this is Captain Chuck. And Chuck, this is my brother-in-law, Blake. I'm sure you've heard me talk about him?"

They shook hands. "I've heard Cassie sing your praises, Chuck. Thanks for watching out for her down here."

"I'm afraid I wasn't around when the infamous Jack Crum came calling that day. I sure wish I had been."

"Me too, but I heard that her knight in shining armor rescued her."

I kicked him in the shin. "Blake!"

He laughed, but then sobered up. "And that's who we're worried about right now. Have you heard that he's missing under strange circumstances?"

Chuck looked at me with concern. "Yes, Gil told me. Have there been any new developments?"

"Not that we know of."

"Gil said that things looked kind of suspicious in the boat so the police had been called. Don't worry, if they're involved, I'm sure he'll be fine."

"I sure hope so," I said, "but they didn't seem too concerned. I got the feeling they thought it was just a scuffle and Carl had gone off to sulk. But that's not like Carl. He's not the sulking kind. That's more like me." He and Blake both laughed. I started to tell him that the Coast Guard had been called, but I didn't want any more rumors started at the dock.

"I'm really worried about him, Chuck. I think you realized before I did, how I feel about Carl."

He smiled. "It was written all over your face, Cassie. I wondered when you were going to give in to it."

I tried to smile, but it just didn't make it past my lips. I'm sure my eyes told the real story. They always do.

"It took me a while to really know how I felt. And now he's gone and I can't tell him how much I care for him." Tears were beginning to form in my eyes. "To tell you the truth, I didn't know what to think of him and I still don't. He's so mysterious and for a long while, I thought he was into something illegal."

Blake looked surprised. "Why didn't you tell me? I would have moved you and Eleanor out of here in a heartbeat."

"Blake, I know better now. He's got too big of a heart to be a bad guy. I know even good guys can make mistakes, but I truly don't think Carl would do anything illegal."

Chuck shook his head and looked sad. "Cassie, even good guys can sometimes be persuaded to do bad things for money. They get greedy."

My self-righteous, indignant ugly self almost shone through, but I contained it...mostly. But I did stand a little taller and held my head up in the air. "But Carl's not like that! I know it in my heart!" Then I softened. I hate it when I do that, because then I cry. Not a full force cry out loud kind of cry, but I couldn't help the big tears that filled my eyes and ran down my cheeks. What had happened to big tough Cassandra Phillips? She never cried.

Big brother Blake stepped in. "Chuck, it was nice to meet you. I'd love to hear your stories sometime about your job, but Cassie is set on taking the boat out for a little while and I promised I would go with her. As you can see, she's quite hurt about this whole situation."

"Cassie, I'm so sorry," Chuck said. "I wouldn't want you hurt for anything in the world." He looked stricken and I rushed to assure him.

"You didn't say anything to hurt me, Chuck. The tears come and go so easily since I've been sick. I'm not usually like this."

"But you're upset, and I wouldn't have...."

"Shush," I said. "When Blake gets me out on the water, I'll be fine. It's my happy place." I started walking toward my boat.

"Okay, goodbye, Cassie," he said. I turned around and waved. It seemed strange to not see a big smile on Chuck's face. I could tell this business was getting to him too.

CHAPTER 24

Carl:

Now that I knew there was another guy on the ship besides Big Boy and Harvey, I would have to act with caution. I had been aboard small freight ships before and I tried to remember the layout of boats such as this. Normally the sleeping quarters were on the top deck behind the cabin, and the cargo areas below, so for now I felt safe. I could handle one person at a time if they came down to check on Harvey, but if they both came down together I may be in for trouble. Flare guns are not like a normal gun, in that you can only load one flare at a time, so it's time consuming to reload. I hoped I wouldn't have to use a flare at all. I've never actually seen anyone shot with one, but the training videos tell it all, and it's not a pretty sight. If shot close range, it can catch a person's clothes on fire and go from there. Of course, visualizing myself being thrown to the sharks was not a pretty sight either, so I figured if I had to use it, I could.

Where were Sean and Brent, I wondered? They had to know something was wrong when I missed my check-in call. When they couldn't reach me by phone or radio, their next step would be to go to the dock, then seeing my boat there and not finding me home, they would start a search, hopefully.

I mentally thought through the guidelines we used in comparable situations. The ship had not yet moved to the coordinates I gave them, but it wasn't far from it and they could do a perimeter search calling in other vessels if needed. The next step would be to call in for a helicopter visual. Maybe they were already out there waiting for backup. It would make more sense. Bringing a helicopter in close when illegal activities are involved is dangerous for the pilot and copilot and anyone else aboard the copter. I thought about our motto, the Coast Guard motto. *Semper Paratus*, meaning always ready, and I knew they had to be out there somewhere ready to make the bust and rescue me. And they wouldn't give up on me.

I looked around the ship. It was small by cargo ship standards. The pilot cabin is usually in the front, but this one was designed with a center cabin with the cargo areas on the front and back. On the back side where I stood, there was a canopy partially covering the lower deck where the shipping cartons were stored. The canopy's purpose was to disguise the cargo on the ship in case a plane spotted it from the sky, but it was serving my purpose well by blocking their vision to where I stood below deck. But it also prevented me from seeing any stirrings around on the top deck or who was in the cabin.

I knew I needed a plan of action, but my brain and body didn't seem to be in sync. I was burning with thirst, I was nauseous, and every swell of the waves made my head feel as if it would explode. All I wanted to do was lay down under the stairwell and sleep. I reached in my pocket. Goody Powder is my best friend. It works for just about any kind of pain. I pulled it out along with something else. It was the frosty blue piece of sea glass that Cassie had given me the night we went to watch the sunset. I remembered the night well. It was when I first knew I was in love with her. I had told her how beautiful she was, and she laughed it off. She doesn't know how attractive she is, but it's not only that, it's her wit, her sweet nature hiding behind her past hurts, and yes, even her temper that draws me to her. It would never be boring living with her. Her ex-husband must have been a jerk. No wonder she has trust issues.

The Goody powder wasn't doing me a lick of good without water, but the seaglass and the thought of Cassie's vulnerability gave me the stamina to stay awake and try to stay alert.

Just then, I heard the engines start up. We were moving. I knew something was bound to happen soon.

CHAPTER 25

Sean:

"I haven't seen but two people on board since the shrimp boat left. And they're both in the cabin," Brent said, as he pulled the binoculars away from his eyes.

"So you haven't seen any sign of Carl?"

"No, but I imagine they've got him locked away somewhere." The big "if" was out there, but we didn't voice it. What we both were thinking and didn't have the nerve to say was "if he's still alive".

I took the binoculars from Brent and scanned my eyes over the ship again. We were in Carl's boat and I was sure we hadn't been spotted. We were far enough out, and the blue-green camo color of his boat works well for undercover work on the water. The radio in the boat had been jerked out when we found it at the dock, but we had an extra one in the truck and when I drove the truck up to Gray's Landing to meet Brent in the boat, we quickly installed it. You can never count on cell phone service on the ocean.

Brent finally spoke the unspeakable. "I don't think they would risk killing him, would they? It's one thing to be charged for drug trafficking. That'll get them a good ten years, but murder will get them a lifetime in jail, or the death penalty."

"But it's so easy to get rid of the evidence out here. If they threw him overboard, we'd never find him."

"If Carl's conscious, they'd have a hard time throwing him overboard."

"Yeah, but we never dreamed that he could let himself get kidnapped either. He's about as canny as they come."

"They must have caught him when he was unaware anyone was on to him," Brent said.

I thought about it for a moment. Carl was always aware of his surroundings. His mind must have been elsewhere. "He's in love, Brent. Women can do that to you. That's why I keep telling you to never let yourself fall in love, especially when you're working a case like the one we've been on for the last few months."

Brent looked at me in disgust. "But Carl knows that too. Why would he go and do something stupid like that."

"The heart is a mysterious thing. Before you know it, a woman has got you hook, line and snuckered. You just wait, you're young. It'll happen to you someday."

He smiled. "Schm..., I like playing the field too much. There are too many women out there for me to get, as you say, 'snuckered'."

"That's what I thought too, and here I am with a wife and two kids."

"That'll never happen to me."

He sounded so sure of himself, I had to laugh. But we were in a no laughing matter situation. Without seeing any signs yet of Carl, I was worried.

"When are we going to move in?" Brent asked.

"You know what our instructions are. Just as soon as the cutter gets here. It should be any minute now." I looked to the east and thought I saw a speck of white but I couldn't be sure, so I scanned the horizon with the binoculars. "Yep, there it is. It's moving in right now." I handed Brent the glasses.

Our method of operation is always to go further out to sea and move in from the east. If they're a novice, they'll expect us to be coming from the west and we can get right upon them before they know it. And I'm thinking these guys are novices. They've just made too many mistakes so far. But if they're not, our cutters can outrun them any day of the week.

Brent jerked me out of my thoughts and to the matter at hand. "Look! The ship's moving," he said, handing me the glasses again.

I looked, and sure enough, they had steered the vessel around and were heading south. Our radio was already tuned into the private channel reserved for the Coast Guard, and I pushed the button and spoke into the receiver, "Target is moving to the south. Permission to follow?"

"Go ahead," was the response. "We're close behind you but staying out of sight until you say ready."

We were ready, like our motto, *Semper Paratus*.

It was apparent they didn't know we were behind them, because they moved out slowly and never picked up pace. We drew closer, but came to the conclusion they weren't even looking for trouble - a sure sign they were not experienced drug runners. That made me feel a little better. Maybe they wouldn't be so callous about taking someone's life. Or then again, maybe they thought they were safe since they had Carl. He would never give his identity away or let on that there was a sting operation on to them. The gang we had reckoned on would slit your throat in a heartbeat. If we only knew who we were dealing with! Brent kept the binoculars trained on the deck while I took the wheel.

"Hey, I see someone."

"In the cabin or somewhere else?"

"There's still just the two men in the cabin, but I see someone stirring around on the back deck. Oh my gosh! He's waving at us, Sean. It's Carl!"

He took over the steering wheel while I took the binoculars. I couldn't tell who it was, so I moved the diopter and adjusted the focus. It was Carl and thank God, he looked unharmed.

"Stay directly behind the ship, in its wake until we get closer. We're out of their line of vision. Then we can drift to one side or the other. Stay on the starboard side where all the crates are. The crates, plus the way the ship's designed will keep them from seeing us come close. I'll notify the cutter to be prepared to move in, in case we need help."

The cutter signaled they were prepared, and I took up the binoculars once more. I could see Carl motioning to the starboard sign.

"Go ahead, Brent. Make the move to the right. He's trying to tell us something."

As we got closer, I could see where he was motioning. Brent saw it too.

"A rope ladder! How convenient. Have they just turned him loose on the lower deck? Apparently they don't know who they're dealing with".

"I don't think so. I have a feeling he somehow escaped and they don't know it yet. Pull up as fast as you can and run alongside them until I can grab hold of the ladder. If just one of us can get up on deck, we can help him. I'm sure he doesn't have any kind of weapon."

"Here, you take the wheel and I'll climb the ladder. I'm younger and you're better at steering these little boats in tight quarters than I am."

"I'm not going to argue with you on that. But I won't be far behind you. I'm going to tell the cutter to move on in, and after you get on deck, I'm grabbing hold of the ladder and ditching the boat. That'll be three of us on board in case there are more than two people."

"That's a little risky, isn't it?"

I laughed. Brent was still a Seaman. I was a Petty Officer and Carl, a Lieutenant. "Everything we do is a little risky, wouldn't you say? You just volunteered to go up the ladder."

He grinned. "I'm ready when you are."

I pulled up right beside the ladder. It wasn't quite long enough. "Here, tie this rope to it to make it a little longer."

He did as he was told. Adept at his rope tying, he easily made two more steps. Then he pushed off without a word. I kept up the pace and when he made it to the top, I shut the motor off and grabbed the rope. The boat was left behind as I climbed the ladder. Brent pulled me up over the railing and we both ran for cover. I didn't like what I saw when I reached the top. Carl looked bad. He was sitting on what appeared to be the ship's emergency box under the stairwell. I kneeled beside him and tried to evaluate his condition. His eyes were dilated and he was feverish. We needed to get this over and get him to a doctor.

"How many are on board?" I asked.

He smiled. "Three, if you count the one locked up in the cargo area over there." He pointed to the latched lid on the deck.

"Have they missed him?"

"No, they think he's in his cabin, drunk. But I have a feeling, they'll be looking for him soon. It's been over an hour."

"What do you suggest? Should we go to the upper deck and try to take them by surprise?"

"No, I had planned to get them one at a time if you guys didn't show up. I figured one of them would come down looking for Harvey after they didn't find him in his cabin. I was going to attack him first, then go after the one in the cabin."

"With what? You're not in any condition to attack anyone."

"With this." He pulled a loaded flare gun from behind the box.

"Touche. That would put him on fire."

"It was all I had." He barely got it out, and was looking weaker by the minute. I took my jacket off and rolled it up in ball and put it on the floor beside the box.

"Here, you lie down beside the box. Brent and I will handle the rest."

"Are you kidding?" he said. "I've been waiting all afternoon for this."

Just then we heard someone walking on the upper deck and a loud voice booming, "Harvey, where are you? Drunk again, I'll guarantee you. Get your sorry self up here."

We all froze in place.

CHAPTER 26

Carl:

When I saw my blue boat closing in on the ship, I wanted to shout. I was holding out hope they would come. I couldn't believe the guys on the upper deck hadn't seen them, especially since they knew my boat. Harvey must have been their normal lookout. I had known they would eventually come down to look for him and as weak as I was, I was afraid I couldn't have handled either one of them.

It was a relief when Sean and Brent climbed aboard. After we talked for a few minutes, we heard someone at the top of the stairs.

I whispered, "Ya'll go around behind the stairs and circle to the left as he comes down. He'll turn this way looking for Harvey. I'll come out to meet him. You two take him from behind."

"Like he did you?" Sean was grinning.

"Yeah. I can't wait to see his face. Go on."

The boys did as I asked, and sure enough, the brute started down the steps calling Harvey, this time using lots of profanity. He got to the bottom and just as I figured, he turned to the right - the direction where Harvey's last orders from the captain had been to go throw me some food. As he took his first step round the corner, I stood out from the stairwell holding the flare gun, cocked and waiting. His reaction was priceless. He held up his hands and backed up.

"Well if it isn't the big boy who likes to hit from behind," I said, talking in a much more commanding voice than I felt capable of.

"Where's Harv?" he said, looking around.

"We traded places," I said. "He was looking for a dark place to ride out a hangover and I was looking for a boost up."

He backed up even more. "Wh-what are you planning to do with that thing?" he said, pointing to the gun.

"Same thing you were going to do with me. Yeah, I heard your plans for me as you walked up the steps after seeing the captain off."

I was enjoying every minute of watching him squirm, but was wondering what was keeping the boys. "I'm going to make you shark bait", I said, waving the gun back and forth, "but I figure the sharks might like you better a little toasty and well-done rather than rare."

"Aw, I wasn't really going to do that. I was just runnin' my mouth. The cap'm would'a had my hide."

He looked around the deck and I could tell he was looking for an escape opportunity. He was trapped and willing to take a risk. I was afraid he would call out to the other man in the cabin. Sean must have sensed it too, because at that very moment, he and Brent stepped from the shadows and came up behind him. I watched as Sean grabbed him from behind and jerked him around. Brent gave him a smashing blow to the right side of his head and he fell to the deck, knocked completely out....

Brent smiled. "That's what he did to you, isn't it?"

"Yeah, I would have liked to have done it myself, but I don't have the strength left in me. Thanks."

"Any time. Let's get him tied up and gagged. Don't want him alerting the other guy, do we?"

Just then, we heard the crew member running toward the stairway. "Get back," I said. The boys pulled our man easily to the back of the stairwell.

"Bates! Hurry back up. There's a Coast Guard cutter coming in from port side. What do I do?"

Sean had the deepest voice among us, more like the man laying at our feet. "Make a run for it," he said. "I'll be right up."

"Okay," he said, and we heard the feet pounding in the other direction.

"It's time we made our grand entrance into the cabin," I said.

Brent looked me over. "I think you should stay here with our captive in case he wakes up. I don't want to have to pamper you while we're raiding the cabin. You look like you're about to keel over."

As much as I wanted to be in on the action, I knew he was right. "Go ahead then. I'll finish tying up old Bates here so he won't give us anymore trouble."

As they headed up the stairs, I worked on the ropes, tying his arms behind his back. I found some duct tape in the box to put across his mouth and wrapped it around his head. It was somewhat disturbing that I found great pleasure in knowing how painful it would be to get that tape off. He had certainly not had any sympathy for me, but an 'eye for an eye' isn't usually my style.

I heard a ruckus from above and then the engines shut down. A few minutes later Sean was shouting down the stairs, "We got him!"

I looked up and watched as Sean and Brent came into sight.

"The last one," Sean said, as he held the man halfway over the railing. "We're coming down." Sean had his arm looped under the man's arm and Brent followed with his revolver in his back.

"Meet Nathan Cummings," Sean said as he stood in front of me. I had heard of Cummings before, just as I had heard of Walter Bates. Two of the most notorious drug runners on the Atlantic, who made numerous trips bringing cocaine and marijuana in from South America. Normally, someone much smarter in the ways of the drug trade would arrange to bring the drugs up the coast by ship, and each time they successfully slipped away. There had been several near misses, but finally we had caught them. They had gotten away so many times before, because they had a bigger and smarter crew. Poor old Harv had a drinking problem. They never should have trusted the lookout position to him.

The excitement of a successful bust made it all worthwhile - even the pain. But this would be the last Hasta La Vista for me. Thirty years with the Coast Guard.... I had joined when I was a mere nineteen-year-old kid. It was time to retire, especially after the challenging job the past few years of being undercover in the drug trade.

I pulled the blue seaglass out of my pocket and rubbed the polished glass. Like the glass, I had been tumbled around by the sea long enough. I was ready for a new mission, a happily ever after one.

The cutter pulled up beside the ship and six crew members boarded, quickly assessing the situation and taking charge. Their mission had been to find me, and knowing there was reason to believe I had been hurt, a medical officer was on board the cutter. Sean didn't waste any time getting me transferred over to be examined.

"You should change clothes, old boy. You smell like a mixture of dried blood, throw up and motor oil."

"The motor oil turned out to be a lifesaver," I said.

"How so?"

"It made my hands slippery enough to get out of the ropes."

As I was changing into a work uniform, the doctor came in. "Not so fast," he said. "I need to examine you before you get completely dressed."

"What's the verdict?" Sean said, as I lay on the cot with the older physician giving me the once over.

"Yeah, what's the verdict, Doc?"

"You've got a concussion and you're severely dehydrated," he said. "You'll feel better after we get some fluids in you. Then we'll take you back to Wilmington for a CT scan."

"I'll get a CT scan later," I said. "Go ahead with the IV to pump some fluids in, but I have some unfinished business to take care of."

I needed to talk to the boys about the one who got away. "We need to get back to the dock at Wenona's Place. I have an arrest to make. Sean, can you ask Mitch to get the cutter going so we can find my boat?"

"I suppose so, since I'm the one who ditched it."

"Yeah, you know how I feel about that boat." I was kidding and he knew it. I did love that boat, but it wouldn't have done me a bit of good if I had ended up being shark bait.

But we had to get busy. If news got out about me being rescued, the shrimp boat would be long gone by the time we made it back.

"At least wait ten more minutes to get this last half pint of fluid in you." The doctor adjusted the settings on the IV. "And drink plenty of water on the way. Between the concussion and the dehydration, you're going to need it."

"I guess we have ten minutes to spare."

"Wait a minute, I'll be right back." Sean walked away. In a few minutes he came back. "We'll be underway any minute now. Two of the crewmen are staying on the ship with our prisoners and they'll steer it back to port. The three of us will get aboard your boat and take it to Gray's Landing where I left the truck. You and I will hurry on to the dock and Brent will meet us there in the truck in case we need help. Who is it we're after anyway?"

I heard the engines start and felt the forward motion of the cutter. I could answer Sean's question later. I only had about ten minutes to lay back and rest. It had been a long day.

I heard Sean say as I drifted off to sleep, "I'm calling Cassie. I promised her I would."

CHAPTER 27

Blake was already in the boat and had the motor running when I hopped in. At least it would give us something to do other than wait. I think Blake realized that too, but he asked me once more if I was sure I wanted to take the boat out.

"I can't just sit here," I said. "Just ride me around a little bit. Let's go up through the inlet here. It meanders around in a maze of swamp grass. You can go a couple of miles in and around and never lose sight of the dock when the tide's high. It's low right now and the grass is higher, so we won't be able to see our way back. Just remember the turns or we'll be stuck back here until the tide changes."

"I'm not good at directions," Blake said. "Why don't you draw a map of the maze as we run it?"

"Good idea." I reached in the small dash and pulled out a notebook and a pen, my stash in case I get inspired to write, which I usually do on the water.

After about twenty minutes of wandering through the maze, I asked Blake to stop. He'd kept his promise to be quiet.

"Do I need to throw out the anchor?" he asked.

"No, we're only about four feet deep here anyway. If we drift, that's fine, but it's pretty still right now. The tide should be changing soon and we'll start drifting back in."

I opened the side compartment and took out my bamboo fly rod and reel from its pouch. It's a three-piece rod that Daddy gave me for my birthday one year, and I quickly assembled it. I had some artificial shrimp in my tackle box so I baited the hook and cast it out. "Gil says that flounder get pulled back here on the high tide and hang around on the low tide until it comes back in again. I'm going to try for a big one." I smiled, and Blake smiled back. We both knew that it really didn't matter if the fish were biting. Just having a rod and reel in my hand was enough.

I finally decided I wasn't going to catch a fish. They just weren't in the mood for plastic shrimp and I didn't blame them. I pulled my cell phone out of my jacket pocket. There were no messages. I tried once again to call Carl. There was no longer an option to use voicemail. It just rang one time and quit.

"Is your phone on?"

Blake pulled his out. "Yep, nothing."

"Blake"?

He put his phone back in his pocket and looked at me. "What is it, Cassie?"

"Let's use the map coordinates and see if we can find Carl." I looked into his eyes pleadingly. "We just can't sit around and do nothing."

"Cassie, we would only get in the way. Besides, your little boat isn't safe to take out in the big water."

I sighed. "I know. Just wishful thinking. Let's go back in, then. Maybe someone's heard something and Eleanor hasn't gotten wind of it yet."

He didn't say a word, just turned the key and the engine started right up. "I'll lead us back in," I said. Keeping an eye out for the twists and turns was something to occupy my mind. As I gave Blake step by step instructions as we rounded each bend, I realized I hadn't counted on the fact that pondering in a quiet place, even if it's the place that makes me happiest, would make my imagination run in overtime. So much for relaxing.

When we pulled up to the dock, Eleanor came down to meet us.

"Any news?" I asked. She shook her head, no.

Blake tied off the boat from the front and I had just reached the rope at the back when my phone rang. I was so clumsy reaching for it in my pocket, I almost dropped it, but on the third ring, I answered.

"Cassie?"

I didn't recognize the voice. "Yes, who is this?" I asked.

"It's Sean. I told you I would call when I had some news to tell you."

I sank to my knees right then and there on the dock. "Please tell me he's alright."

"He's...." The connection was lost.

"He's what? Hello. Hello, can you hear me?" I started bamming the phone on the deck. I knew it was pretty stupid, but I couldn't help but remember my Daddy always bamming the top of our old TV when he couldn't get good reception, and it was the only thing I could think of to do.

Blake came running over and grabbed the phone out of my hand. It's a good thing. I would have probably thrown it in the water, I was so frustrated.

"Who was it? What did they say?"

"It was Sean and all he said was, I told you I would call when I had some news. When I asked if Carl was okay, the connection was lost."

Blake looked at the number showing on the screen and tried to call Sean back. It rang once and the connection was lost again.

Eleanor put her arm around me. "Cassie, I don't think he would have called unless the news was good. Otherwise, he would have waited to give bad news in person. You know yourself how fickle the cell phone service is out in the ocean. He'll call back when he gets a stronger signal."

"She's right, Cassie, but we'll keep trying to call this number back. It sounds like it won't be long until we find out. At least we know that Sean is one of the good guys."

"I hope so," I said. "Unless he's trying to get some ransom money for Carl."

Blake laughed. "That's the doom and gloom side of you coming out, little sister. Let's think positive."

Doom and gloom? When had I been doom and gloom? Was this how I had appeared since my divorce? Oh Lord, was I going to have to change my whole outlook on life? Get out of my comfort zone of 'I'm a failure'? Maybe it's time.

***

I sat in the gazebo and strained my eyes looking for Carl's blue boat. Fishing boats had been steadily coming in since about six o'clock, those on board hungry after a day of fishing. Blake had gone out for a pizza and we ate pretty much in silence, none of us very hungry. Earlier, the tourists had been in and out of the seafood houses buying fish or shrimp for a fresh seafood evening meal. Life was going on as usual on the docks, but I was dying a little bit inside as the clock ticked away.

The Black Jack trawler was docked at the Clarks' dock, but I hadn't seen him, nor did I want to. I wasn't afraid of him knowing that Blake was around.

Chuck had said he would be going out later in the evening and I watched as he made preparations on the trawler. About every fifteen minutes, he would sit on the old wooden bench that backed up to the ice house and try to make a phone call. I thought he must be trying to call Red or Johnny. They hadn't shown up yet, and I knew he would need deck hands if he was going shrimping. I hollered down to him, and he jumped as if startled. Apparently he couldn't see me inside the gazebo with the sun right behind me and so low in the sky. He put his hands up to shade them, and then shouted back.

"Hey, any word?"

"No, not yet. I'm trying to stay positive since Blake thinks I'm gloom and doom." I stood up and leaned over the railing. "I saw you making a phone call. You tryin' to call the boys?"

He looked confused.

"Johnny and Red. They are going out with you, aren't they?"

"Oh, no, not this time. I'm picking up a crew north of here where I'm shrimping. Since I'll be working up that way, I won't be getting back here as often. Red's girlfriend isn't crazy about him being gone that long and

Johnny's got him a full time job now. The auto repair shop where he was working part time lost one of their mechanics and offered him the job."

"Well, good for him. I'll miss seeing him around though. And you? How long will you be gone?"

"I'm not sure yet. Depends on how the shrimping is up there."

"You leaving tonight? You ought to wait 'til morning. That's a long ride in the dark."

"It's not so bad. The weather's good and I don't mind riding at night."

"Good luck. I hope you'll be back before we leave for the summer."

"Me too. If not, I hope to be here the next time you come on vacation."

I heard my name and turned around. Blake was yelling, trying to get my attention.

"Cassie, come quick. A truck is pulling into Carl's driveway."

"I'll see you later, Chuck." I took two steps at a time, hurrying to see what was going on. Blake had already gone out front when I reached the gazebo, but Eleanor was waiting for me.

"Come on," she said.

Just then I heard a familiar sound coming from the waterway. It was a boat coming in and I could tell by the sound of the engine it was Carl's.

"Listen," I said. Do you hear that?"

"No," she said. "What is it?"

"It's Carl's boat. I don't know who's driving it, but there's no mistaking the sound of that engine." I saw

Chuck boarding the trawler, and I called out to him. "Chuck, that's Carl's boat coming in!"

He called out, "I'll be seeing you Cassie. I'm pulling out. There's too much commotion going on and I don't want to be any later leaving."

"Have a good trip," I said, and waved to him before he went inside the cabin. His engines started, drowning all other sounds.

Blake came running around the corner of the house and climbed the steps to the gazebo.

"I don't know who drove up, but whoever it is took one look at the dock and turned the truck around. He's parked down there now."

I was breathless from going up and down the steps so many times, but I was anxious to get back on the dock before Carl got there, if it was Carl driving the boat. A feeling of disappointment returned. What if it was Brent or Sean coming to tell me something had happened to Carl? I would wait here until I saw who was in the boat.

As we watched, the blue boat came rounding the corner from the waterway, and there was the most beautiful sight I'd ever seen. Carl was sitting on the bench seat and one of the other guys was at the wheel. I waved my arms wildly but they didn't even look. They were going way too fast and I was worried they would run into the Lady Lu when Chuck pulled out.

"Watch out!" I shouted, and just as I thought, they rammed right into the trawler. "Oh my gosh," I said. "They crashed the boat!"

Chuck had been right. There was too much commotion going on. He should have left earlier.

CHAPTER 28

Blake, Eleanor and I watched in confusion. I wanted to run down to the dock to see Carl, but Blake stopped me.

"Not now, Cassie. Something's going on that we don't need to get in the middle of. You know he's safe, so let's leave it at that for now. We can watch from the safety of the deck. When things calm down, I'm sure we'll hear what's going on."

I knew he was right. I just couldn't imagine why Brent ran into the Lady Lu. Was he trying to get away from someone chasing him? Was he on drugs? A gazillion questions were going through my mind, when another large boat pulled into sight from the waterway side.

"A Coast Guard cutter," Blake said. "You girls stay here. I'm walking down closer to the dock. When I find out something, I'll come back and tell you."

As soon as he left, I started walking down the steps from the gazebo to our dock.

"Cassie! Blake said to stay here."

"Blake's not my daddy," I said stubbornly. "Besides, I'm just going down the steps. The ice house is blocking our view."

I turned around and looked at Eleanor as she sat there looking helpless and worried. It made me feel guilty that I had spoken to her harshly. I wouldn't even be here; I wouldn't have met Carl if she hadn't rented the little house to help take care of me. Of course, maybe it would've been better to have never met him at all if he was in trouble with the law. I couldn't allow myself to even think such a thing, though. There had to be an explanation for all this madness. Then it occurred to me. Jack Crum! It had to be him - he was the one in trouble. The Coast Guard must be getting ready to arrest Jack, and maybe Carl was the hero who had reported him.

That buoyed my spirits and as soon as I reached our dock, I scooted myself up onto the fish cleaning station and tried to see what was going on. The cutter had docked and several of the crew members were unboarding. They were all dressed alike. I had always thought of them wearing white, but as I watched them jumping onto the deck, they were wearing dark blue t-shirts and work pants. Maybe the white was for dress uniforms. Then I spotted Carl standing beside Chuck's trawler. Dang, he was dressed just like the others. What was that all about?

And what the heck was he doing? He had Chuck in handcuffs! My good friend, Chuck. There must be some mistake! I jumped down from where I was seated and took off running down the dock. I got near the ice house and Eleanor called me.

"Cassie, what are you doing? Come back here."

I looked back at her but kept running. "They're arresting Chuck," I said. "He hasn't done anything wrong. I've got to stop them. They should be arresting Jack Crum."

Just then, my foot hit something wet and cold. As my feet slipped out from under me, I realized someone had spilled ice from the ice house and there wasn't a single thing for me to catch onto. I felt like I was in a slow motion movie as I slid right up to the edge of the dock and started my fall into the water. Muddy, icky, low tide, fishy smelling water. Way to go, Cassie, I thought, as I made the splash. So much for making a graceful entrance!

The next thing I knew, someone had thrown me a rope. I looked up into the most exquisite pair of blue, blue eyes. He was laughing. It made me forget all about my mission of saving Chuck from the handcuffs.

"You're a sight for sore eyes," he said, never taking his eyes off mine.

"It's not funny, Carl," I managed to say as I was spitting water out of my mouth.

"Grab hold of the rope. I don't know how we're going to get you up." He was looking around the dock when Brent came up carrying a wire fish basket.

"I got this off the trawler," he said. He looked down at me. "When I drop it down, get in and we'll get you out."

I sighed. Perfect. I've always wanted to be pulled up in a fish basket.

Carl was still laughing. "If you were going to jump in, Cassie, you should have at least jumped in on the other side. The water's much cleaner over there."

I scooped up a handful of the murky mud and threw it at him. He ducked. "Not on my clean clothes, you don't." As the wire basket settled in the mud, I climbed in. He and Sean had no trouble pulling me up on the dock and when I climbed out, Carl grabbed me in his arms and held onto me. My arms went around his waist, neither of us caring about the mud. So much for his clean clothes.

"Uh, I'm out of here." Brent was blushing and practically ran back to the boat.

I pulled slightly away from him, remembering why I had gone running down the dock. "What's going on, Carl? Why were you handcuffing Chuck?"

"It's a long story, Cassie. I know how much you like him. I did too. He's a nice guy - just got mixed up in something he shouldn't have. Money does strange things to people. We'll talk about it later when we get you cleaned up."

I leaned into him, trusting him fully. The story didn't seem important anymore. I just wanted to feel his warm arms around me.

"I was so worried about you," I said.

"It's all over now and I can tell you everything. But not right now." He pulled me tighter and I didn't object.

He nuzzled my neck, the only place on me not covered in mud. "I missed you, Cassie. All I could think of was wanting to get back to you. That's what kept me going."

My heart turned to mush as those beautiful blues met mine. I loved this man; I had never been more sure of anything in my life. But I didn't dare tell him. It would jinx everything.

CHAPTER 29

The next day, I slept until almost noon. I had spent the wee hours of the morning trying to piece together all that had happened on the dock that night as I tossed and turned in my bed. When I finally slept, I dreamed that Carl was holding my hand and someone was pulling him away from me, and finally succeeded in breaking our grip on each other. It was so real, I could smell the scent of his aftershave lotion. In the dream, I made one final lunge to grab his hand back and woke up just in time to keep from falling off the bed. His pillow was still on my bed and I held it close, this time falling into a dreamless sleep with his comforting scent surrounding me.

Carl had slept late too, and I saw him only briefly before he had to make a run to Wilmington to finish processing the federal paperwork and meet with the authorities. Blake had found out from Sean that Carl had a concussion and would be getting a CT scan in Wilmington too.

People on the docks were naturally curious about what transpired with the Coast Guard, so I stayed inside to keep from answering questions, only going out when I saw Johnny and Red drive up and walk out on the dock. Chuck's shrimp boat was still docked, but it was marked off with yellow tape and there was a federal marshal aboard doing a thorough search, stopping only to occasionally sit in the cabin and watch the people on the dock. I watched as Johnny walked up to the boat and asked the marshal a question. He pointed to our house and I waited on the gazebo as they walked up our stairs. I talked to them for quite a while. I tried to answer their questions, but I still had so many questions of my own.

***

As it turned out, I found out that Carl's last name was Wright. McGee was his undercover name. And I didn't even find that out from Carl. Of all things, I found out by visiting Captain Chuck in prison.

Carl didn't think it was a good idea, but at my insistence, he took me to Wilmington to see him. He had already been arraigned and had pled guilty and would be sent to Raleigh the next day. He was cooperating with the authorities and hopefully would get a lighter sentence when the case finally came to trial. It would be in Federal Court. Drug trafficking is a serious offense. Carl said Chuck had never had so much as a speeding ticket before, which is why they never suspected him at all. He had been pretty sure it was Jack Crum heading it all up and couldn't believe it when he heard Chuck's voice from under the stairwell of the cargo ship. Jack had enough trouble of his own, though. It turned out that Harvey and the other guys on the ship had been dealing with Jack for quite some time, and they were singing like canaries to try to lighten their own sentences. Frank Osborne, the person they suspected from the beginning, hadn't been involved at all.

I was curious about how and who purchased the drugs in the first place. Carl said Chuck had bought the shipload of marijuana from Mexico and it was transported up the coast by Bates and his crew. At night while we were all sleeping, Chuck would load a few bales on the trawler and bring it in, going up the narrow channel to a warehouse he had rented, not far up the river from our rented houses. He would unload them and go back out a few days later and do it all over again until he had emptied the ship except for a few bales left on the boat that were sold them to one of his buddies from the Chesapeake area, a boat called the Iron Gate. The buyer for the large quantity in the warehouse had already paid Chuck and had just started emptying it, when they caught him in the act.

Carl said if it had been anyone but Chuck, they would have caught on to it before they did. They were stumped when neither Crum nor Oswald made any moves toward the ship. They didn't have the slightest suspicion that it was Chuck. Just like me. I would have never believed it if I hadn't watched it unfold.

I almost cried when I walked into the visitor's room and saw Chuck in an orange jumpsuit. He looked sad and embarrassed when he saw it was me visiting.

"Cassie, I'm so sorry you have to see me like this. And even sorrier for what I did and that I disappointed you. Can you ever forgive me?"

"Can you forgive yourself?" I asked. "Chuck, you were the last person I would have believed to be mixed up in something like this, but I didn't come here to judge you. You were such a good friend to me and helped me get through the worst of my chemo days. Is there anything I can do for you?"

"Well there is one thing. Johnny. He's a good kid, and he looked up to me, and I'm worried. Everyone in his life has let him down. Would you ask Carl to go by and see him sometime, try to keep him on the straight and narrow? There's so much I could have done with that boy, but Carl can help him if he will."

He was having trouble looking me in the eye. I was quiet until he finally looked up. "Chuck, what made you do it?" I wanted to know.

He hung his head. After a few minutes, he answered.

"I let myself get greedy. Just one time and I would be done with it. My daughter was about to lose her house and I wasn't making enough money to help her. I borrowed money on the trawler, but it wasn't enough, so when those sleazebags contacted me, I said, why not. I could buy the drugs cheap and sell 'em for street value. It would be enough to pay my loan off for the trawler and pay off my daughter's house. I'd seen others do it back in the '70's and get rich. I had a warped way of thinking about things. That's what greed does to a person."

"And now your daughter's not any better off and she's lost you to a jail cell," I said. "You're not doing her a bit of good in here."

He sighed. "I know. I've even lost my shrimp boat. They confiscated it as part of the penalty for what I did. Won't do them much good though. It's mortgaged for all it's worth."

"Don't worry about Johnny," I said. "I've already talked to him. He came down to the dock when he heard what happened. You had more influence on him than you thought, in a good way. He just seemed worried about you. Said, he understood how people could get caught up in things that were not right. Said he'd done it himself but got help just in time."

"That boy has grown up in a hurry. I'm glad to hear he's got his head on straight."

"Carl told me you tried to make sure the other guys didn't hurt him when he was on the ship. I want to thank you for that. How did you figure out he was the undercover guy?"

"I didn't at first. The other guys got suspicious when they noticed that the blue boat showed up too many times to be coincidental. And you've got to remember, Carl was thinking Crum was behind it all, and wasn't careful enough to notice that he was getting too close to the real enemy. But they still never knew who Carl was, even after they caught him. They just thought he was a snoopy tourist who had seen too much. When I saw that it was Carl that they had hit over the head and brought to the ship, I sure wasn't going to tell them he was Coast Guard. They would have killed him for sure."

"But how did you know?"

"When he first came down for the summer, I tried to figure out where I had seen him before. About a week ago, it came to me. I remembered I had seen a picture of him on the back cover of a book I read several years back - a book that he wrote. I didn't think it was a coincidence that he was here. That's when I hurried to try to get things tied up and over with, before he caught on that it was me." He paused. "But it didn't work out that way, did it?"

I shook my head, no. "But what gave him away?"

"The book was written in the '90's so he's changed a lot, but the eyes gave him away. I remember thinking all those years ago how blue his eyes were in the photo. Tell him if he ever goes undercover again, he needs to wear some brown contact lenses or something."

I laughed. "Yeah, the eyes are what hooked me, too. Did you say he wrote a book? He didn't tell me that! What kind of book?"

"It was a book, a true account book about drug smuggling along the East Coast as far as I can remember. I remember at the time thinking how stupid those people are who think they can get away with something like that. Never thought I would give in to it myself."

"Ah! That's the book I found in his house. That's what made me think he was a drug smuggler." I thought a minute. I had looked at the author's name. "Carlton Wright! Carl is Carlton Wright."

"Yeah, and he's a good man, Cassie. I don't hold it against him for arresting me. I was breaking the law and he was just doing his job. During the whole affair, I was eaten up with guilt. If I'd just listened to my conscious, I would have quit before I got so involved and turned it over to the Coast Guard. They would have caught the head man and I would'a been a hero." He laughed wryly. "Always wanted to be a hero. Now I'm a jailbird."

"I wanted you to be a hero too, Chuck. You were to me. But there's no going back."

***

I couldn't hide my tears when I came out of the visiting room. Carl was waiting for me, but didn't tell me 'I told you so" like Stan always did when I went against his wishes. We walked outside and he held the door open for me to get into his truck. He closed the door and got in on the driver's side. He didn't start the engine, he just turned toward me and took my hand.

"I'm sorry you had to see him like that, Cassie."

"That's what Chuck said, and he has so many regrets." I looked up and he was watching me. It reminded me of something else Chuck had said. "And he told me something about you too, Carl." He looked confused. "Or is it Carlton?"

"Oh, that..."

I grinned. "Yes, that. Carlton Wright - not Carlton McGee after all. And why didn't you tell me you had written a book?"

I was teasing him, but I don't think he realized it. His look was a cross between guilt and remorse. "You don't know how much I wanted to share everything with you, Cassie. For you to think I was some sort of a despicable character was killing me. Since I've been working undercover, I've tried to keep my work and social life separate, but as fate would have it, I met you while I was on the job trying to establish a new identity." He stopped for a moment, then looked at me and smiled. "You did think I was an unsavory character, didn't you?"

"To be honest, I didn't want to, but I did. But you were the best kissing unsavory character I'd ever met, so I was torn."

He laughed. "So you've kissed unsavory characters before?"

"I'm afraid so; I married one. I take that back; he turned into an unsavory character when he cheated on me."

"That's another reason I hated deceiving you. You already had trust issues from being married to that guy, and here I was deceiving you too."

"It's different," I said. "I can see that now. If I had known the full story, I could have made it more dangerous for you." I stopped talking abruptly as a thought hit me. "You know, I trusted Chuck so much, I would in all probability let it slip what you were up to, and that would have been disastrous! It would have ruined your chances of making a bust. Oh my gosh, I see the importance of it now."

"I'm glad you do. Does that mean I'm forgiven?"

I leaned over and gave him a lingering kiss. "Does that answer your question?"

"Not quite," he said. "Let's try it again."

A few minutes and some rapid heartbeats later, someone knocked on the window. Embarrassed, we both looked up to see who it was. It was Sean, holding a file folder full of papers. He motioned for Carl to roll the window down and when he did, Sean was grinning like a Cheshire cat.

"You're making a spectacle of yourselves. If you're going to make out, do it somewhere besides the prison parking lot."

"Oh, yeah," Carl said, looking around. "I momentarily forgot where we were."

"I can see that," Sean said. "I'll pretend I didn't see you. Carry on." He gave Carl a thumbs up signal and walked away.

He gave me one last quick kiss and cranked up the truck. "Hold that thought," he said. "We'll pick up where we left off when we get back to the house." He put the truck in gear, but then put it back in park. He turned back around to face me. "Or do you want to see where I really live? It's not too much out of the way on our way back. I live in Southport."

"Maybe another time. I think we should go back where we'll have chaperones," I said, laughing. "I'm not sure I trust myself or you."

He put his hand under my chin and turned me to face him. "Cassie, I would never rush things. You've been through way too much for me to take advantage of you. I want you to take time to really get to know me. I mean, you didn't even know my real name until today. I care about you too much to ever hurt you."

My hand trembled as I reached up to touch his face. There were only two other people in my life who had felt that way about me. My daddy and Eleanor.

***

That evening I was exhausted and went to bed early. I was so thankful that my nausea hadn't returned after my last treatment. When I called Simon to ask him about it, he said that the extreme nausea I felt after the first treatment in Wilmington was more than likely a result of the stronger dosage of chemo or it could have been caused by a viral infection. Chemo patients have a compromised immune system and are more susceptible to infections. But with the newest formula change, I should be feeling much better. And I was better, and thankful that I wasn't dealing with nausea during all the emotional trauma of Carl's kidnapping.

For the next few days, Carl and I spent most of our time together either lounging on the beach or going for long boat rides. We had a lot of catching up to do. He was easy to talk to and I found myself confiding in him. All my bottled up feelings I had carried since Stan and I divorced seemed to melt away. I should have fallen in love sooner. It would have saved me a hefty psychiatrist bill.

And as he promised, he told me all about his job and all the missions he had been on since he had been assigned to work undercover. He tried to downplay them, but I knew, based on this most recent event, the danger he must constantly be in.

"That's scary," I said. "Now I'll always be worried about you."

"Maybe not anymore. When I was in Wilmington, I talked to my Captain about retiring."

"That's a relief. But how can you retire so young? And I can't see you sitting around all day watching TV."

He laughed. "Do you sit around all day and watch TV?"

"That's different, I'm a writer."

"Well, I didn't plan on just doing nothing," he said. "Actually, he talked me out of it."

My face fell. "So you'll still be in danger?"

"That's the good part. Did you know that the Coast Guard operates under the authority of Homeland Security?"

"I remember hearing something about it. But of course I didn't know anyone in the Coast Guard at that time, so I wasn't too curious about it." I smiled. "But now I am."

"They're opening up a satellite office in Charleston, and he thinks he can pull a few strings and have me working out of there. Not under the Coast Guard, but Homeland Security in a contractual position. What do you think?"

What did I think? I thought it was time for me to sell my house in Raleigh and move back to the old home place on Calibogue Sound so I could be closer to Charleston, but I didn't tell him so.

***

Sunday morning rolled around, and he finally got to keep his promise to go to church with me, and as we walked in, we got the same warm welcome from Wilbur and his wife as Eleanor, Blake and I had received the

Sunday before. I had been apprehensive about going, thinking that we would be asked lots of questions. The drug smuggling was the talk of the town, but inside the church was all about worship and no mention was made of it and no judgements were handed out.

Carl held my hand during the whole worship service, squeezing it at times when the message seemed just for me or for him. It felt like my heart was being squeezed too and I thought to myself that I didn't deserve to be this happy, but by the end of the service, I realized that God was giving me a second chance and I shouldn't question His plan for me.

We spent the afternoon with Eleanor, laughing, playing cards and accusing each other of cheating. But the weekend had to come to an end, and the next morning was back to Wilmington for me and Eleanor, and off to Raleigh for Carl. He was to be in on the interview and questioning of Chuck, and this time it felt good to know where he was. I thought back to all those weeks of worrying and wondering. If I hadn't been so completely enamored with Mr. Blue Eyes, I never would have stood for it. As a matter of fact, Eleanor and I had talked about that very thing in the car on the way to Wilmington.

"This time last week, I was all stressed out because I had no idea where Carl was." We had just crossed over into New Hanover County on Highway 17 North. "And I was practically convinced he was up to no good."

"And I had no idea you were so obsessed with him," she said.

"It wasn't obsession," I argued. "There's a difference between obsession and being in love."

She laughed. "Not much. I remember when I fell in love with Blake, it was like an obsession. He was all I could think of."

"Would you have loved him even if you thought he was a criminal?" I asked.

"Probably," she said. "There's no room for reason when you're in love."

"Why am I just now finding out this stuff? You should have told me a long time ago. When I was getting ready to marry Stan, you should have said, 'Would you marry him if he was a criminal' and I would have said, heck no, I'm marrying him because of his money. It would'a saved me a lot of headache and crappy feeling days."

She laughed so much I thought she was going to cry. She finally settled herself down. "It wouldn't have mattered what I said, Cassie. You thought you were in love with him and you were so hard-headed, if I had told you, you would've gone off and eloped and broke your daddy's heart."

"Daddy should have told me, darn it. He didn't like Stan from the get-go."

"Mama did, though. She wanted us all to marry into money. She told me when Blake and I got engaged that she was disappointed he wasn't rich, but at least he had a good education and could make something of himself."

"I hadn't thought about that. I was just happy that I had pleased her for a change by marrying a man she liked. She was a hard one to please."

"Yet, she loved us. I never felt unloved, did you? I just felt that I had to try harder to make her happy."

"I guess so," I said. "She just had a different way of loving, I suppose." I turned to her. "Thank you, Eleanor."

"For what?"

"For insisting that I let you take care of me. And for bringing me to a place for some peace and quiet. I'm glad you didn't take me for some wild adventure." We both laughed together.

"If this hasn't been a wild adventure, I'd hate to see what you call wild."

"And I would have never met Carl. I don't know what will come of it, but even if nothing does, it's been the best couple of months of my life."

"And however horrible your cancer diagnosis was, you wouldn't have met him otherwise."

"God must have a weird sense of timing and a warped sense of humor," I said.

We had reached the clinic. She turned off the ignition and turned around to face me.

"Have you and Carl talked about the future?"

"Heavens no. He may be moving to Charleston which would give me an even greater incentive to move back into the old home place where I would be close to him. We've gotten to know each other a lot better this week but I still think we should take things slow. Honestly though, Eleanor, can you imagine me living with someone after all these years? And why on earth would anyone want to marry someone whose chances of living are less than 70%? He's already lost one wife."

"Cassie, your treatments have been successful so far. You can't act like you're dying. And remember what I just said about there being no room for reason when you're in love? If he loves you, he'll want to be with you."

"I can't even hope for that, Eleanor. I know he cares for me, but I don't think he's ready to make any kind of commitment."

"We'll see." She opened the door. "Let's get you inside. The quicker we get this day over with, the better. Then you'll just have one more treatment and after next week, it's back to Charlotte to see Simon again."

"Hallelujah! Let's get this done!"

I thought about what Eleanor said as the poison was pouring through my body. Did I dare hope?

CHAPTER 30

Eleanor and I made it back home Tuesday morning. My blood tests that morning showed that my white blood count was slightly low but not enough to worry about. They would skip the shot, hallelujah! Just one more week of this; I was counting the hours and the days. But what would happen after I went home? Would Carl still want to see me? Would the miles between us be a deterrent and our romance wane?

I decided I wasn't going to be Miss "gloom and doom" as Blake had insinuated I was, and I would make the best of every minute I got to spend with Carl. He came back from Raleigh on Wednesday and came over to see me as soon as he returned. He filled me in on all that happened in Raleigh.

"This is a first for me," he said. "I'm usually on a high when we close a case with multiple arrests, but I've got no satisfaction at all on this one. I hate it when a good man makes a mistake that will stay with him forever."

"I know what you mean. But you can't let it worry you. He had a choice and he made the wrong one."

"Come over to the house with me," he said, taking my hand. "We'll put on a sappy movie and hold hands and eat popcorn."

"Do you have popcorn?"

"No."

Do you have any movies?"

He looked sheepish. "No."

I laughed. "Do I have to bring everything?" I pulled a box of microwave popcorn out of the cabinet and went to the living room and picked out some movies. "Do you have a DVD player?"

He laughed. "Yes!"

"What are we waiting for?"

***

The next few days went by in a blur. On Thursday, Simon called. He had arranged for me to have my last treatment in Charlotte on the next Tuesday. He had set up my scan for the 30th. Eleanor reminded me that our rental on the little white house was just through the 31st so we would need to have everything packed and ready to check out on Monday since we were planning to head on to Charlotte that afternoon. All the while I had been planning to have a full week to spend with Carl, when in reality now I only had a few days. I had to remind myself over and over not to wallow in pity, but to enjoy every minute.

On Friday, we went by boat to Southport. He wanted to show me his house. He had a permanent boat slip at the waterfront marina, and as we unboarded the boat, we were greeted by several people.

"Do you know someone who can give us a ride?" I asked.

"It's just a short walk." He grabbed my hand. "This way."

His house was a small cape cod just two blocks from the waterfront. All the houses on the street were shaded by huge live oaks and I fell in love with the little town immediately.

The house was decorated in a nautical theme and was full of antiques. The hardwood floors sparkled and I commented on how clean it was.

"I can't take all the credit," he said. "I'm gone so much it would get dusty if I didn't have someone come in and clean once a week."

"It's just the kind of place I expected you to live," I said. "I love how close it is to the water. What will you do if the job comes through in Charleston?"

He laughed. "I would find a place to rent down there until I see if I like the job and the location. I'll keep this place in the meantime."

"So would I," I said. "It's beautiful here so close to the water."

"I always knew I would live near water," he said. "It's in my blood."

I smiled, and wondered how many times I had said those words, yet I had allowed Stan to take me all the way to Raleigh to live and I had never really been happy there. I should have moved back to the Lowcountry when he and I divorced, but I just never made the effort. I would remedy that soon.

***

Monday came around quicker than any of us wanted. Blake had brought the SUV to pack up Eleanor's things to take back home. I had only come with one suitcase full of clothes and a few personal belongings, so I didn't have much to pack. Blake left on Sunday to take Eleanor's things on back to their house and would meet us in Charlotte on Tuesday. After my scan on Thursday, they would go back to Mount Pleasant and I would stay with Simon a day or two longer and drive my car on back to Raleigh. It was depressing and I dreaded saying goodbye to Carl.

His rent was up at the end of the month too. He told Blake he would be lost if he were to stay on after we left. He had one more trip to Raleigh on Wednesday, then he would go back to Southport. I gave him my address in Raleigh just in case he was still there when I drove back from Charlotte on Saturday. I would miss this place and miss knowing he was right next door when I wanted to see him.

We invited him over to share the last of our breakfast food on Monday morning. Eleanor heated up the last two frozen waffles while Carl and I finished off what was left of the cereal, fighting over the last few cups of milk. As Eleanor cleaned up the dishes we spent the rest of our time together sitting on the Gazebo. We were both in a somber mood.

"Penny for your thoughts," I said.

"They're all of you," he said. "Just worrying about your scan and what it's going to reveal."

"It's been on my mind too, but worrying isn't going to change the outcome."

He leaned across the table and took my hand. "I love you, Cassie."

Any other time, I would have been thrilled to hear those words from him, but I knew they were said out of sympathy. I waited for a moment to try to control my emotions.

"Empathy and compassion shouldn't be mistaken for love, Carl. You've been so kind to me, even when you've driven me crazy with your disappearing acts. I've loved having your shoulder to cry on."

"So you love my shoulder to cry on, but you don't love me, is that what you're trying to say?" He looked hurt and his blue eyes were fixed on mine. I struggled to know what to say. I did love him, but I didn't want him to feel trapped after saying things he didn't mean, just because we were going our separate ways. I felt tears stinging my eyes, and he reached up to wipe them away. "You don't have to answer me now, Cassie, but I'm not going to let up on you until you do." He lifted my hand to his lips and kissed my fingers, one by one.

He got up from the table and pulled me up out of my chair. He hugged me tenderly, and regretfully, didn't try to kiss me again. "I'll be in touch," he said, and turned to walk away. I wanted to go running after him and tell him how much I loved him and to come back and kiss me proper.... But I let him walk away and I knew I would live to regret it.

CHAPTER 31

Eleanor and I arrived in Charlotte late on Monday just as the afternoon commute traffic was dying down. Simon wasn't home yet, but Joan gave us a warm welcome. She had dinner warming and the smells from her kitchen told us we were in for a treat.

"It's a traditional Japanese dish," she said. "Of course I have Americanized it somewhat to suit Simon's tastes."

"What's it called?" Eleanor asked, while lifting the lid from the large skillet on the stove.

"It's Kakuni, a braised pork dish. It's cooked in water and sake, along with soy sauce, ginger and fresh leeks. My mom always served it on cabbage, but Simon likes his on rice, which is how we're having it tonight. We'll have a cucumber and tomato salad for a side, and a traditional banana pudding, southern style, for dessert. Simon's favorite."

"I heard my name," Simon called from the door. He had come in the front door unnoticed as we were drooling in the kitchen. "I don't have to ask what's for dinner. I could smell it when I walked in the door."

He put his briefcase down on the bar stool and gave me a hug first and then moved on to Eleanor. He reserved the best hug for Joan, and it's easy to see that my brother is still as smitten with his wife as he was the day he married her.

During dinner, Simon told me that he had a change of plans for my treatment.

"I've decided we'll forgo the chemo tomorrow," he said. He was all smiles. "Does that suit you?"

"Heavens, yes," I replied. "But why?"

"There's no good reason, other than I just have a good feeling about it. Friday, I called in a colleague to look at the last scan with me. It's a possibility that what appeared to be remnants of the tumors could in fact be scar tissue from scraping the abdominal wall. I've moved up the date of the scan for Wednesday and he's going to study it with me. Two sets of eyes are better than one, and he's just finished extensive training in reading scans for our new equipment."

Was this a glimmer of hope? I decided not to get too optimistic until the time came. I've found over the years that optimism can set you up for disappointment. Gloom and doom Cassie to the very end.

***

Blake arrived on Wednesday morning and drove us to the imaging center. Bert, the same young man as before was the technician on duty and took me back without having to wait. He checked my blood sugar and then inserted the IV. I had brought a Louis L'Amour book with me to read, but dozed off after about ten minutes. Louis's campfires and rivers to cross on surefooted horses usually hold my attention, but this time, I conked out after the first chapter. Of course, I've read and reread all of his books until I almost know them by heart.

I was relaxed when it came time to put me in the time capsule, as I like to call it. I actually slept and only woke up when I heard Bert's voice. "Cassie, wake up. You must be dreaming because you're wiggling around. Stay awake now and try to be perfectly still." I wanted to ask him if I snored, but I was afraid he would say yes and I would be embarrassed. It wasn't long before I was dressed and ready to go back to the waiting room, but first I needed to go to the restroom. It would be a while anyway before Simon and his colleague, Dr. Parker finished reading the results.

I stood at the mirror over the sink and looked carefully at the person staring back at me. I could tell I had gained a little weight back because my cheeks no longer had that refugee look. My complexion was a healthy pink instead of the pale sallow look I'd had since my cancer diagnosis. With a new haircut, I might look halfway decent, I thought. I ran my hairbrush through my hair and checked the brush as I had done every day since I started chemo. For some reason the hair loss had escaped me, and I was grateful for small favors. I dug around in my purse for lipstick and found a bright red. Nah, it clashed with my pale pink blouse, so I opted instead for a tinted lip gloss. I squared off my shoulders and walked out the door. I was ready for whatever my doctors found, or hopefully, didn't find. I stopped at the vending machine, put in a dollar and out popped a Diet Coke, no longer chosen because of the sugar content, but out of habit. Was I supposed to eat or drink after the scan? I couldn't remember. What could it do, kill me? I took a big swig but when I rounded the corner to the waiting room with my mouth full of soda, I gasped and almost spit it out.

There, sitting between Eleanor and Blake, as if he were part of the big happy family, was Carl. My Carl. My blue-eyed Carl who had told me he loved me and I had dismissed his feelings, thinking they were purely sympathetic. He hadn't seen me yet. I looked good and hard at this man I had fallen in love with. His eye color was such a contrast to his dark brown, almost black hair. It made his eyes appear even bluer because of it. He was lean and fit, not quite six feet tall. His nose was slightly crooked, his chin had a faint dimple and to me, he looked better than all those cowboys in the Louis L'Amour movies combined. Tom Selleck, yeah, a lot like Tom Selleck who played one of the Sackett brothers.

Eleanor looked up as I was watching him intently. "There she is." She jumped up and ran to me. "How did it go?"

"I think I snored," I said. "Bert made me wake up."

"I hope you sleep on your left side," Carl said. He was still sitting in the chair and made no move to get up.

"What?" I asked. "What has my left side got to do with snoring?"

"Because I sleep on my right."

Blake laughed and Eleanor blushed. They seemed privy to something I wasn't.

"I have no idea what you're talking about," I said, and at the time, I really didn't. "What are you doing here, anyway?"

"Well, that's a nice way to be greeted," he said. "Eleanor called me to tell me they had changed your scan date, so I came today instead of Friday."

"I didn't know you were coming at all. I'm sort of in shock."

"I have to admit, I was expecting a bigger welcome."

I looked around. There were several people in the waiting area and they were all looking at us. "Carl, there's a room full of people in here."

He surveyed the room. "Oh, I see them now. My eyes were only for you." He smiled, making my heart go into a tailspin. "Well, let's go outside then." He took hold of my arm at my elbow. "Excuse us, please," he said as he led me to the double doors leading outside. "The lady and I have something to discuss." There was a murmur of laughter as we walked out the door.

He calmly led me down the sidewalk, to the side of the building and to the parking lot. As soon as we rounded the corner, he took me in his arms and kissed me, not some wimpy kiss, but a big fall in your arms, dazzling kind of kiss. A kiss that I was so completely absorbed in that I begged for more as he pulled away.

"There's a bench in that little copse of trees. Let's go talk," he said.

"I'd rather kiss," I said, smiling sheepishly.

"We may get arrested for indecent behavior," he said, laughing at my expression.

The bench was metal with a slatted back and a small metal plate attached to one of the slats. It was a memorial bench given by some doctor's wife in her husband's loving memory. We sat on it anyway.

"You didn't answer my question," I said. "Why did you come here?"

He rolled his eyes. "Did you really think I wouldn't? I wanted to be here with you after your scan. I drove straight from Raleigh."

I sat there with my head down, looking at my hands in my lap, not knowing what to think or say. I was thrilled. Did this mean he really did love me?

"I drove by your house while I was in Raleigh," he said. Why didn't you tell me you lived in a silver palace?"

I grinned and found my voice. I was much more comfortable when we weren't discussing the 'L' word. "Because I didn't want you to like me for my money," I said. "Do you know how many proposals I get on a weekly basis when all the men I meet see my house? It's exhausting." I brushed my hand over my brow in my best melodramatic act.

He laughed. "Don't you get lonely in that big house?"

"So you're making your move too?" I was on a roll and he was amused, playing along with me.

"No ma'am," he said, seriously. "I only marry for love."

I swooned. "Oh, in that case, I'll sell all I own and give it to charity and we can live happily ever after, but broke, in our cozy little nest by the sea."

His blue eyes met mine and he was no longer laughing. "I would like that," he said.

He looked serious. I tried to slough it off and carry on the game. "I'll bet you say that to...."

"Cut it out, Cassie. I'm serious."

"You are?" My heart was beating so fast, I was worried I would have a heart attack in the middle of the medical plaza. At least I would have someone to do CPR.

"Yes, I am. I tried to tell you on the gazebo, but you wouldn't listen. I love you."

He was serious. I could see it in his eyes. I could see the mirrored image of how I must look to him with the love and longing in my own eyes. But what if.... I voiced my concern. "But what if the scan results are bad? What then?"

"Good or bad, Cassie. It doesn't change what I feel for you. I'll show you the meaning of 'in sickness and in health'."

Neither of us had seen the small group walking toward us until Simon spoke. "There you are. We were looking for you." Blake and Eleanor were right behind Simon and Dr. Parker, and they were smiling.

Carl jumped up and reached for Simon's hand. "You must be Simon. I'm Carl Wright. Cassie and I were just out here discussing our wedding plans."

"Carl!" I stammered. "We were...." I stopped. Blake and Eleanor were hugging each other and Simon looked from me to Carl in confusion. Dr. Parker looked amused. He seemed to understand before me or Simon did.

"Well, don't you want to know what we found out today?" Simon said, still reeling from Carl's news.

Carl sobered up. "Yes, he said. Yes we do."

Simon looked at me. "Cassie, there's the HIPAA law you know. Is it okay to discuss your medical condition with this... with Carl?"

All of a sudden, I knew there was good news. There had to be! The man I loved was in love with me.

"Yep, Simon," I said. "If the man wants to marry me, by all means tell him the good news or the bad. It may change his mind."

Relieved that I wasn't being coerced into marrying someone, Simon lightened up and smiled. "Cassie, from all we've seen today, you are cancer free."

Carl wrapped his arms around me and we both laughed. Eleanor interrupted our hug with one of her own and Blake wormed himself in to hug me too.

Simon was finally catching on. "When's the big day?" He asked.

Carl looked at me. "It's your call, Cassie."

I looked at Eleanor. She nodded.

"I happen to know a good preacher who lives less than an hour from here," I said, thinking he would back off a little.

The way he looked at me told me he was right there with me. "Call him and see if he can marry us tomorrow."

"I'll need a new dress, and Eleanor will too."

"Let's make it Sunday afternoon", Eleanor said. If I know Rock, he'll want some counseling sessions with the two of you."

Blake laughed and shook Carl's hand. "I hope you know what you're getting into?"

CHAPTER 32

The dresses had been bought, the marriage license purchased, and frayed nerves were settled. Carl had just walked out of the pastor's office and I had just walked in. I put the books I had borrowed from Rock on the coffee table and looked around. It was our first marriage counseling session. Rock's secretary, Reva, had treated me and Carl like long lost family when we came in the door, such a sweet but sassy lady. I knew that she and I were cut from the same mold the minute I laid eyes upon her.

I was a little nervous, like I was sitting in the hot seat or something. The door was open to the outer office and I could hear Carl chatting with Reva. I took a seat in one of the two chairs facing Rock's desk. He looked so cool and collected, like he did this every day. My chair scraped the floor as I scooted it up a little closer.

"I thought marriage counseling was something you do when your marriage is in trouble, not when it's ready to begin," I said as I fingered the leather piping along the chair's arm.

"Unfortunately, that's what a lot of people think," Rock said. "Christian counseling for couples before they marry is important. It gets you off to a good start. Just as I'm doing with the two of you, I prefer to talk to you separately and then together."

"Carl was in a good mood when he came out," I said. "So you didn't talk him out of marrying your wife's crazy aunt?"

He laughed. "I didn't even try. He's head over heels, and he's got his heart in the right place. He's a good man."

I sighed. "I know he is. I just hope I can live up to his expectations of me."

"He doesn't seem to have any lofty expectations, Cassie. I think you'll both do just fine." He glanced at the books I had put on the table. "Did you have a chance to read those?"

"Yes, I did." I picked up the book about the apostle John. "I had never read John from start to finish. He spells it out, doesn't he?"

"Yes, he does."

I laughed nervously. "So, you're not going to test me on the book, are you?"

"Of course. We're going to have a pop quiz." At my panicked expression, he laughed. "Just kidding, Cassie. The Bible isn't meant to be a test. It's a guide for living. Especially the New Testament."

"I do have a favorite verse in John."

"Which one?"

"It's John 8:36. *'If the Son sets you free, you will really be free'*."

Rock didn't say anything. I guess he was waiting for me to explain, so I continued.

"I feel like I've been set free. Free from some of the things I didn't even realize were consuming me. Like the fear of dying of cancer, and the bitterness that lingered long past Stan's betrayal. And that deep down feeling that I would always be alone because I was afraid to love again. Somewhere along the line I had lost my faith. Thank you,

Rock, for helping me get it back." I smiled. "Maybe now, I won't be called 'doom and gloom Cassie' by my brother-in-law."

He smiled. "It wasn't me. You were asking all the right questions. I just pointed out where you could find the answers." He stood up and motioned me to stay seated. "I'll go out and get Carl to come back in. I think we're ready to talk to you both together."

My dress was a pale pink summer sheath, and Carl had borrowed one of Rock's suits which turned out to be a perfect fit. The ceremony was simple. Eleanor, Blake, Simon, Joan, and Liz were all there as we spoke our wedding vows and as Rock pronounced us man and wife. I was surprised it was over so quickly.

"You may now kiss the bride," Rock said.

I looked around. All eyes were on us. "With everybody watching?" I asked.

Rock nodded. "That's the way it usually goes."

Carl's smile was tender. Our eyes met, our hands touched and sparks flew. "Ouch." We said it in unison.

He turned to Rock who was watching in amusement. "I think we're in for some electrifying times," he said, "but we'll have the rest of our lives to get used to it." With that said, my Carl, my Mr. Blue Eyes gave me a kiss I wouldn't soon forget.

The End

EPILOGUE

The setting sun is casting golden ripples upon the ocean as we make our way out of the Lockwood Folly channel on the Intracoastal Waterway. There's a light breeze and the salty sea air settles on our wire-rimmed glasses causing the wide horizon to appear hazy. It is only thirty-two miles along the coastline to our first destination where we will spend the night in our cozy cabin cruiser. We want to take it slow and easy, watching as the sun dips down from the sky and sinks slowly into the ocean. The soft, fluffy white clouds are rimmed with gold, much like the antique dinner plates Eleanor inherited from our grandmother. The ocean is a tablecloth, to be shaken out and smoothed flat, but it never seems to be free of its rippling wrinkles. An island of content lies before us, our troubles are long past.

The boat ride from Calibogue Sound to Lockwood Folly and back is a pilgrimage we take at least once during each summer, when the days are long and hot and the only relief is the cool ocean breeze during the evening. When there's nothing on the agenda for tomorrow. On nights of the full moon, the light never seems to be extinguished, only dimmed, turning the ocean black, then lighting it back up with silver. The ocean once again calls out to us, to enjoy its beauty now, in the present. I think about my mother's song, the one that seemed to permeate the soft sea air with her loneliness even though she was surrounded by a passel of kids. I sang it for Carl the first night we walked on the beach and was suddenly aware that I could become my mother and be absorbed by my loneliness. The moon is no longer melancholy for me. Instead, it's a bright light in the sky filled with hope and love. I'm reminded that God's grace is sufficient.

We're adventurers, Blue Eyes and I. We've learned to listen to our hearts and not our heads. We've learned to shuck off our independence and lean on each other. We laugh, hold hands and sing funny songs as we glide through the backwaters. We talk of the plans and dreams of our youth that were put on hold because of failed marriages or demanding jobs. We give the dreams a name, write them down and then weed out the ones that are no longer important to us. But there are still many; special ones that we put in a small tin pail and call it our bucket list. I once thought bucket lists were for the very old, but they are also for survivors which we both are. The written words on little slips of paper look like a daunting task, but we promise each other not to stress if we don't complete them all. We pluck them out, one at a time, to go on some lark or another; because we know that someday in the far away future, we'll be stuck on the one we're doing now, sailing into the sunset.

79785328R00148

Made in the USA
Columbia, SC
29 October 2017